Please don't wake

Her breath stilled when stir. Josephine peeked over her shoulder at the bed and let out a startled gasp. Sebastian lay with his head propped in his hand—wearing nothing but a lazy smile.

So much for sneaking away unnoticed....

"Going somewhere?" he asked, his voice thick from sleep.

"I didn't want to disturb you." She sat on the edge of the mattress.

He chuckled. "Sure you didn't." His dark hair was mussed and his smile went from lazy to cocky. He looked far too tempting for a woman filled with morning-after regret.

"Umm...I have to water my plants." The excuse was lame and they both knew it.

He reached for her fingers. "We have a problem, Joey."

"Great deduction, counselor."

"I want to make love to you again."

She sighed. Forget that he was technically her boss—he was smart, sexy and dangerous. The kind of man who could break her heart. The kind she could easily fall for—*hard*.

Dear Reader,

Secrets. Everyone has at least one. Some are fun and meant to be shared. Others are so dark, revealing them could cause a whole host of troubles for everyone. If you've been keeping up with THE MARTINI DARES miniseries, then you know there are plenty of secrets in the Winfield girls' world. And the secret that Josephine "Joey" Winfield learns in *My Guilty Pleasure* is one that can shake the very foundations of the lives of the people she loves the most—her sisters.

The skeletons falling out of the Winfield closet are only the beginning of Joey's problems. She has another secret to contend with, a true guilty pleasure, when she has what she thinks is a one-night stand with her boss, hotshot litigator Sebastian Stanhope.

My Guilty Pleasure was a fun story to write, one I especially enjoyed because of the opportunity of working with Lori Wilde (*My Secret Life*), Carrie Alexander (*My Front Page Scandal*) and Isabel Sharpe (*My Wildest Ride*). I'd love to hear from you! Please write to me at jamie@jamiedenton.net or visit my Web site, www.jamiedenton.net.

Happy reading,

Jamie Denton

Joey's Amorétini
1 oz vodka
1/2 oz Chambord raspberry liqueur
1/2 oz pineapple juice
Shake well with ice, strain into a martini glass and enjoy!

MY GUILTY PLEASURE
Jamie Denton

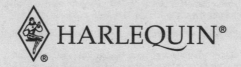

HARLEQUIN®

TORONTO • NEW YORK • LONDON
AMSTERDAM • PARIS • SYDNEY • HAMBURG
STOCKHOLM • ATHENS • TOKYO • MILAN • MADRID
PRAGUE • WARSAW • BUDAPEST • AUCKLAND

ISBN-13: 978-0-373-79374-7
ISBN-10:   0-373-79374-X

MY GUILTY PLEASURE

www.eHarlequin.com

Printed in U.S.A.

ABOUT THE AUTHOR

Jamie Denton surrendered a longtime career as a legal assistant to pursue her passion for writing when she sold her first novel to Harlequin Books four days before Christmas in 1994. Since then, not only have her books appeared on bestseller lists, but she is also the recipient of several notable awards. Jamie's passions extend beyond writing on occasion. In those rare moments away from the computer, she enjoys refilling the creative well with gardening, knitting or cross-stitch. She can even be found curled up with a good book. (What else but a romance?) Her spoiled-rotten purebred Somali cat, Cookie, is usually nearby, too, snoozing or demanding affection. For more information about Jamie or her upcoming books, visit her Web site at www.jamiedenton.net.

Books by Jamie Denton
HARLEQUIN BLAZE
10—SLEEPING WITH THE ENEMY
41—SEDUCED BY THE ENEMY
114—STROKE OF MIDNIGHT
     "Impulsive"
141—ABSOLUTE PLEASURE
166—HARD TO HANDLE *

*Lock & Key

For Lori, Carrie and Isabel

_1_

"HEY THERE, BABE. You come here often?"

By the sheer grace of what remaining patience she had left after a particularly rotten day, Joey Winfield resisted the urge to flip the bird at the scruffy biker with the tired old pickup line. She was in no mood for flirtations, harmless or otherwise. She'd come to Rosalie's, a roadhouse located on the outskirts of Boston, for one reason—to blow off some steam. She'd wanted a place where no one knew where she came from, that she was one of "the" Boston Winfields. A place where the whiskey wasn't watered down and where she could get rowdy if she wanted to or just sit quietly and contemplate the bottom of several empty glasses of bourbon. At Rosalie's, no one would judge her every move.

Maybe she'd even kick a little ass at the pool tables tonight. She was in that kind of mood.

She manufactured a saccharine sweet smile for

the biker blocking her path. "Not as often as you comb your hair," she said saucily as she sidestepped the bear of a man and continued toward the bar before he realized he'd just been insulted.

Sidling up to the long mahogany bar scarred with age, she signaled for Mitch, the bartender. Perched on an empty black vinyl bar stool, she hooked the heels of her scuffed cowboy boots on the chrome rung. "Jack. Neat," she ordered when the bald-as-a-cue-ball bartender, who made the scruffy biker look puny in comparison, worked his way down the bar to her.

Mitch's bushy unibrow winged upward at her request, but he didn't offer comment as he set a glass in front of her and poured a generous two fingers' worth of whiskey. Hard drinking was a staple of Rosalie's and Joey had every intention of doing some herself.

She fingered a twenty from the front pocket of her figure-hugging jeans and slapped it on the bar. "Better make it a double." She slid the bill toward Mitch. "And a pack of Marlboro Lights while you're at it."

That unibrow rose another fraction as he snagged a pack of cigarettes from the rack near the register. "Bad day?" he asked, tipping the bottle of JD again.

More like a bad year.

"You have no idea." She took a swig of Jack

Daniel's, then tamped the pack on the bar before ripping it open and withdrawing a cigarette. Her throat would feel like seared meat come morning, but she didn't much care. She had a serious edge in need of smoothing out and could use all the help she could get in that department.

"How's your sister?" About a year ago she'd met Mitch through his sister, Lissa, who'd been a resident of the halfway house where Joey mentored troubled girls. The bald, tattooed bartender was capable of keeping the roughest customers in line but was a giant marshmallow where his little sister was concerned.

"Keeping her nose clean, last I heard," he said, offering her a light. "Phoenix is a good place for her."

"Glad to hear it," she said. Lissa had been a mixed-up kid who'd gotten in with the wrong crowd and ended up in trouble, despite her big brother's efforts to the contrary. She'd served three months in County on an accessory conviction to a B&E, then had been released to the halfway house for the first six months of a three-year probationary period. Joey had been the one to convince Lissa's probation officer to allow the girl to relocate to Phoenix to live with an aunt for a fresh start. It pleased her to hear the situation was working out well for Lissa.

"Anything else?" Mitch asked.

She shook her head and drew on the cigarette. "Thanks, I'm good."

Mitch nodded then took off to answer the call for more drinks from a pair of weary-looking men at the other end of the long bar. She took another sip of whiskey, then glanced around at the smattering of tables. She didn't recognize any of the patrons, but then she wasn't exactly a regular at Rosalie's, either.

She supposed she could've gone to Chassy, the trendy bar on Boston's south side that her half sister, Lindsay Beckham, owned, but she wasn't in the mood to be sociable or hang with the girls. Conversation wasn't high on her list of priorities tonight. In fact, the last thing she wanted tonight was to be Josephine Winfield, born with a silver spoon up her privileged ass. Tonight she wanted to just be Joey, a girl looking to raise a little hell.

Just once she wanted to be herself and not worry about the consequences.

A sardonic smile twisted her lips before she drew heavily on the Marlboro. What a concept, she thought, blowing out a plume of blue smoke. But who did she think she was kidding? She'd been so tied up in being what everyone else wanted her to be, or thought she should be, she'd forgotten what the real Joey was even like. Maybe she never really knew, but one thing she did know with absolute certainty—she was so sick to death of pretending to be the good girl she could scream.

But that didn't mean she didn't enjoy a few minor rebellions on occasion. Like Molly, the high-priced Bengal cat she'd bought because it kept her Great Aunt Josephine and her snooty daughter, Eve, who were both severely allergic, from dropping in on her unannounced. Or the sleek fire-engine red sports car she drove, which made her Grandmother Winfield frown with disapproval whenever she buzzed past the main house to the carriage house, located on the extensive grounds of the Winfield family home. But those were the only acts of defiance her family was aware of…of that she made certain. Her grandmother and great aunt's blue hair would turn a shocking shade of purple if they knew that deep down, their little golden girl, little miss Harvard Law graduate, Josephine "Joey" Winfield was bad to the bone.

Maybe she should think about finding herself an apartment in the city. Despite the lack of real privacy she had by living on the family estate, the problem was, Joey actually liked living in the carriage house. She enjoyed the quiet, especially the view of the beautifully manicured grounds, particularly the English garden. During the warmer months, she often spent her weekend mornings outside on the little flagstone patio with her morning coffee, a toasted bagel slathered with cream cheese and the *Times* crossword puzzle. But Sunday mornings were *her* quiet time, something she looked forward to all week.

Later would be soon enough for quiet time. Tonight, loud was on her agenda. Rowdy, even. There was that crappy day to shake off, after all, and the sooner, the better.

Her day had started out like any other, until Molly had made her run late. Somehow her mischievous cat had managed to jump on top of the entertainment center. The stubborn feline had refused to come down, regardless of the fact she'd spent nearly ten minutes yowling in distress over her predicament.

A run in her nylons and a chipped nail later, she'd driven like a bat out of hell to get to the office in time for a meeting with one of the managing partners to discuss the status of an important case she had coming up for trial. She'd been stunned to learn that she wouldn't be the lead trial attorney in the matter, but instead had been relegated to second chair, working with some new hotshot litigator the firm had spent weeks recruiting to head up their litigation department.

And what had she done about it? Not a damn thing. She'd very calmly expressed her disappointment, despite the fact she'd been seething inside. Not so much as a single forceful objection. Barely even a real protest, for that matter. She'd just sat there, saying nothing about the hours she'd spent preparing the case for trial, drafting motions and interviewing several witnesses, or the time she'd spent prepping her client for what promised to be a difficult cross-examination. She'd done what she'd been raised to do—be the good girl and not make any waves.

Well, she had once. An outrageous tsunami that she doubted she'd ever hear the end of, or stop feeling guilty about. She was a disgrace to bad girls everywhere.

Angrily, she stubbed out her cigarette and downed another swallow of her drink. What she should've done was told Lionel Kane III to take the case and shove it, along with her position at the firm. But she hadn't. God help her, she knew she wouldn't. *Gilson v. Pierce* was an important case and although she wasn't thrilled to play second fiddle to the firm's newest flavor of the month, at least she hadn't been removed from the case. To make matters worse, the managing partner had rubbed salt into an already open wound. Since trial was starting in another week, she'd been told it was up to her to bring the new guy up-to-date.

She hadn't thought her day could get any worse, but she'd been wrong as it continued to spiral downward. The judge had denied her request for bail for one of the girls she mentored from the halfway house who'd been arrested on a possession charge. Not only did Ginny Karnes have to spend the weekend in the county jail, but the nineteen-year-old now faced revocation of her probation, which could result in her serving out the remainder of a five-year suspended sentence behind bars.

Things became even more chaotic when her secretary had gone home sick, having been struck by a particularly nasty flu bug making the rounds of the office. A meeting with one of the firm's clients had gone badly. Then, to top off the end of a really nasty day, an impromptu dinner with her sisters had resulted in the announcement that her younger sister, Katie, and Liam James, Boston's most eligible bachelor, were now engaged.

She took a long drink of her whiskey. Not that she'd ever begrudge any of her sisters a chance at real happiness. She was thrilled for Katie, but her little sister's engagement to Liam only served to remind her that she was still painfully single with no prospects in sight. She suspected Brooke and David weren't far behind on the matrimonial trail, either, for as much time as the two had been spending together the past couple of months.

Tired of feeling sorry for herself, she grabbed a couple of ones from the change Mitch had left on the bar and wove her way through the increasingly growing Friday night crowd to the jukebox. A country ballad blared through the speakers, but she wasn't in the mood for a cryin'-in-your-beer song. Tonight it had to be rock—the harder, the better.

She slid the bills into the slot, then scanned the choices before making her selections. She settled on the latest from Korn along with a few of her other favorite rock bands.

"Excuse me, but I think you dropped this," a deep male voice said suddenly from beside her.

Joey let out a sigh and turned, a "buzz off" comment hovering on her lips, half expecting to find the burly biker again. Instead, she found a stranger with traffic-stopping looks holding up a five-dollar bill between his long, slender fingers.

Bedroom eyes, she thought instantly. Rich, like smooth, dark chocolate. The kind that promised lust and sin, two of her favorite pastimes. The "get lost, creep" she'd been about to deliver immediately evaporated from her vocabulary.

He had the kind of build she found impossible to resist, too. All wide shoulders and lean hips. The kind that held up to the promise of that lush, dark gaze. Better yet, the cocky half smile canting his mouth had her toes curling inside her cowboy boots.

One look at that mouth and her imagination took off like a shot. Despite her foul mood, she smiled.

Mentally, she attempted to calculate how long it'd been since she'd gotten laid. After counting back six months and not coming up with a single memorable experience, her answering smile faded slightly.

Six months? That had to be a record.

For her anyway.

Considering everything that had been going on in her life, both personally and professionally, it was no wonder she'd been lacking in male companionship lately. Her mother had passed away in July after a brutal battle with pancreatic cancer, followed by the discovery of a half sister given up for adoption that she, Brooke and Katie hadn't known existed. Only last month they'd been delivered another shock when they'd learned Brooke, her older sister, was only her half sister biologically. Not that Brooke's parentage made a lick of difference to her or Katie, but they'd still been stunned by the news, especially Brooke. The Winfields, her mother in particular, apparently had more skeletons lurking behind their closet doors than a centuries-old mausoleum had tucked behind its marble walls.

She shuddered to think what might fall out next.

"I don't think it's mine," she finally said. She had a few folded twenties still tucked into the front pocket of her jeans, her AmEx card in her hip pocket just in case and her cell phone hidden in the inside pocket of her suede bomber-style jacket along with her keys. Her smile returned. "But nice try."

His smile deepened, crinkling the corners of those drown-in-me-forever brown eyes. "Too bad it didn't work."

"Maybe you should've made it a hundred," she replied sassily, then headed back to the bar with his laughter ringing in her ears. He had a nice laugh, she thought as she slid back onto the bar stool. Open. Free. Like he used it often.

God, was there anything sexier?

She signaled to Mitch for a refill. A stab of disappointment pierced her when the money-wielding stud didn't follow her to make another attempt to pick her up. Probably for the best. Her plan to blow off steam didn't include sex with an anonymous stranger, no matter how good-looking or intriguing. That reckless, she wasn't.

Or was she?

Using the long mirror behind the bar, she searched for Hunky Warbucks. She finally found him, seated in the rear of the bar near the pool tables. A slow smile tugged her lips again. Lordy, but he was nice. Nice and hot.

Mitch arrived with her fresh drink and she downed half of the fiery liquid in one gulp. "Let me have some quarters for the pool table," she said, tugging another twenty from her pocket.

Mitch obliged, albeit from the look of warning in his eyes, begrudgingly. "No trouble tonight, Joey."

"What trouble?"

His unibrow hiked skyward again over a disbelieving expression. "Yeah, right. The last time you came in here and shot pool you caused a fight."

"Oh, like it was *my* fault those two goons thought I was the prize?" she scoffed. "Just give me the quarters, Mitch."

"Do me a favor and be specific this time if you want to make it interesting, okay?" His hazel eyes narrowed. "No hustling the customers or I'll eighty-six you from the place."

"I never hustle," she said in her best blue-blooded tone as she hopped off the bar stool. She picked up her drink, tucked the cigarettes and a book of matches into her jacket pocket and winked at Mitch. "I just play to win, is all."

2

HER ASS WAS the sweetest thing he'd seen in ages. After having lived for several years in Miami, Sebastian Stanhope considered himself an expert on the subject.

The blonde bent over the pool table and attempted to line up a difficult shot. Curvy, he thought, eyeing that luscious behind. And firm. He'd bet a month's salary that her sweet and curvy and firm ass would fit his hands to perfection.

Sebastian tipped back the beer he'd been nursing for the better part of the night in an attempt to cool his climbing temperature. It proved to be an exercise in futility the minute the sassy blonde bent forward again to take aim and make the winning shot. Damn if she didn't sink the eight ball into the corner pocket like a pro, and look mighty fine doing it, too.

"That's another fifty you owe me, Bose," she said to a rough-looking biker.

All night Sebastian had been watching her hustle

anyone foolish enough to accept the challenge. The woman didn't know how to lose. He liked that.

"Damn, Joey," the big man complained good-naturedly. He slipped two twenties and a ten from the wallet chained to his dirty jeans. "How'd a babe like you get so good at pool?"

"I played a lot in college," she said, pocketing her winnings. "But hey, don't worry—" she chalked the tip of her cue stick "—I'll give you a chance to win your money back."

Bose shook his head and laid his cue over the table. "Nah," he said, "you're too rich for my blood."

A concept Sebastian understood all too well. He might have the Stanhope name, but the family fortune never had been, and never would be, his. What money he'd accumulated, he'd done so the old-fashioned way. He'd worked his tail off, putting in twice the billable hours as most of the other associates in the Miami law firm he'd joined right out of law school, and had hired a damn good broker to build up his portfolio. He wasn't rich by old money, Bostonian standards, but he no longer had to hustle pool games to survive, either.

He finished off his beer and stood. Sauntering over to the pool table, he laid a buck's worth of quarters down on the polished edge of the table.

Bose inclined his head in Sebastian's direction. "Looks like you've got a new pigeon waiting to be plucked."

The blonde looked over her shoulder at him, no doubt to size up the competition. Her blue eyes sparkled with excitement as a slow, easy smile spread across her pretty face.

"You play?" she asked.

He was no pigeon, which she'd find out soon enough. "A little." Not exactly a lie, but hardly the truth. He just hadn't played much lately, in part because it hadn't been necessary to his survival. There'd been a time, not all that long ago, when a wager at the tables had been the difference between sleeping in his car or making the rent.

A definite gleam entered her gaze. "Care to make it interesting?"

He'd expected no less. The woman was a shark at the tables and had to be a good two to three hundred bucks richer in the time he'd watched her play. Not that he suspected she needed the cash. The woman smelled like money, from the expensive cut of her hair down to a pair of high-quality, albeit scruffy, boots. And he'd spent enough time with his nose pressed to the glass to know the difference.

"What did you have in mind?" he asked her.

She reached into her hip pocket and peeled off five twenties. "Interesting enough for you?" She tossed the bills onto the black circled mark on the green felt of the pool table.

He picked up the cue her previous challenger had left behind and tested the weight in his hand. "Not exactly what I had in mind." He circled the table to her side.

She slipped a hank of honey-blond hair behind her ear. "I don't know you well enough for that kind of wager."

He set the base of the cue on the floor between his feet. With his hands wrapped around the stick, he leaned slightly forward, breathing in her scent. Amid the acrid odors of spilled beer and stale smoke that permeated the air, he caught her subtle fragrance, a light floral mixture. Expensive, too. Funny, but he'd pegged her for something more spicy and exotic. "No, but I'd bet you'd like to," he said.

The blue of her eyes darkened, giving him all the answer he needed.

"Arrogant, aren't you?" She angled her cue against the table while she dropped the quarters into the slot and waited for the balls to tumble into the tray.

He plucked the rack from the other side of the table and set it on the felt near the stack of twenties. "See? You're getting to know me already."

She chuckled softly, then started loading the balls into the rack. "Time to put up or shut up."

He slipped his wallet from his hip pocket and pulled out a crisp hundred-dollar bill to match her bet. "Satisfied?"

Her smile was positively wicked, red-lining his libido. She scooped up the cash and set it on the side of the pool table, then removed the wooden triangular rack before retrieving her pool stick. "Your break," she said, as was customary.

He lined up the shot and sent the cue ball soaring across the table. "So you come here often?" he asked above the loud crack. He kept his attention on the scattering balls and watched the four ball roll into the corner pocket.

"Boy, if I had a dollar for every time I've heard that line." She stepped out of his way when he circled the table looking for his next shot.

He took aim on the two ball and missed, distracted by the subtle scent of her perfume. "Better than 'what's your sign?'" But if he were guessing, he'd say a Taurus, or maybe a Scorpio. The tilt of her chin and the glint in her eye indicated a stubborn streak. Not that he was seriously in to astrology, but when he was growing up, his mother had never left the house without first consulting the obituaries and the astrology section of the *Boston Globe*.

"I'll give you that." She took aim and easily sank

the eleven ball. "And, no. I don't come here all that much. You?"

She didn't strike him as the barfly type, but he couldn't help wondering what someone like her was doing in a place like Rosalie's. The place was a roadhouse in the truest sense of the word.

"New in town," he said as she set up her next shot. Another half truth. He was full of them tonight.

"From where?" She sank the nine ball with a difficult bank shot.

"Miami." He inclined his head toward the table. "Nice one."

"Thanks."

She slowly walked toward him, holding his gaze with every step. Damn if he didn't have trouble remembering how to breathe. She bent forward to line up her next shot. Her slender fingers wrapped around the cue and she slowly slid the stick back and forth. His imagination headed south.

He cleared his throat.

She took aim, then missed. "So you get a sudden hankering for a long cold winter?"

He shrugged. "All that sunshine can wear on a guy after a while." He hadn't planned on returning to Boston, but when the offer from Samuel, Cyrus and Kane had come his way, he never once considered declining. Come Monday morning, he'd be the youngest partner on the letterhead of one of the city's oldest and most prestigious firms, and heading up their litigation department. Not a bad gig for a guy like himself.

She made a sound that almost seemed like laughter. "Boston won't disappoint you then."

He leaned forward to line up his shot, then looked up at her. "So far it hasn't."

That wicked smile of hers returned. He shot and scratched.

She laughed again then effortlessly cleared the table, making one difficult play after the other until only two of his solid-colored balls and the eight ball remained. "In the side pocket." She grazed the eight ball and sank it exactly where she'd called it.

"Thanks." She scooped up her winnings and tucked the wad of cash into her back pocket. "Hello, Manolo," she said, her grin widening. "Worthington is having a sale."

"Play again?" he asked.

"Thanks, but no." Her grin wavered slightly. "I really should be getting home. Maybe next time."

She turned and walked away, heading toward the bar. He stared at the gentle sway of her hips in tight denim until his common sense took hold. What was wrong with him? He couldn't let her get away just yet. He didn't even know her name.

He caught up with her by the time she reached the bar. "You think you should be driving?" She hadn't had a drink in at least ninety minutes. Her eyes weren't glassy and her stride had been steady when she'd walked away from him. Honestly, he didn't think driving under the influence was an issue at this point, but it was the best excuse he could come up with under pressure.

"Excuse me?"

He gave her his best winning smile. "Why don't you let me buy you breakfast?"

"Thanks," she said with a shake of her head, "but no. I'm fine."

Yes, she was. Which was exactly his point. "There's an all-night diner across the road. Just breakfast."

She hesitated. He took that as a good sign in his favor.

"Coffee?" he offered.

"Maybe I could use some coffee."

He smiled. "Good idea."

"Hey, Mitch," she called out to the bartender. "You want anything from the diner?"

Smart girl, Sebastian thought.

"No, I'm good," the bartender answered, then looked him over and gave him a hard stare, leaving Sebastian with the distinct impression he'd suffer a severe pounding should anything happen to the blonde under his watch.

"Two eggs over easy. Bacon, crisp. Rye toast," Joey told the waitress.

"Pancakes and eggs for me," her breakfast companion ordered. "With a side of sausage links." He handed the waitress the menus.

Joey admired his long slender fingers and took a sip of hot coffee. "So, you have a name?"

He stirred cream and sugar into his own mug. "Sebastian."

"First or last?"

"First. You?"

"Joey," she said. *Just Joey.*

He set his spoon on the saucer. "I gotta ask. What's a nice girl like you doing hanging out at a roadhouse like Rosalie's?"

She hid a smile behind her mug. "What makes you think I'm a nice girl?"

"You made sure the bartender knew you were leaving with me," he said, then took a sip of his coffee.

"Caution does not necessarily equate to being a nice girl."

"You trying to convince me you're a bad girl?"

She shrugged. "Maybe." Maybe she'd take him

home and screw his brains out. That ought to convince him.

The possibility intrigued her more than it should. Not that a tumble in the sack with him would be a hardship. Far from it. There wasn't much about the man she didn't find appealing. Even his arrogance was sexy.

He chuckled. "I think maybe not."

She tried not to feel insulted. "You don't know me."

"I'd like to," he said, then took another sip of his coffee. "Get to know you, I mean."

And she'd like to get to know him. But then what?

The waitress returned with their meal, saving her from having to conjure up an answer. Still, she couldn't help wondering how long she'd hold his interest. Until he discovered where she came from and became so intimidated by the Winfield name, and all that it implied, that he'd ditch her cold? He wouldn't be the first guy scared off by her family's wealth and reputation. The Winfield name was as old and prestigious as Massachusetts itself. Rumor had it they had roots as far back as the Mayflower. Thanks to her ancestors, and a ridiculous fortune made in the shipping business, she had more money in her trust fund than her grandchildren's children would ever be able to spend.

Or maybe until he realized she wasn't the clingy type and was perfectly content living alone? Or maybe until he learned that aside from her family, her career ranked at the top of her list of priorities?

"Are you allergic to cats?" she asked suddenly.

He slathered butter on his pancakes. "No. Do you like dogs?"

"Very much," she said. Brooke was allergic, but Katie had recently acquired a cocker spaniel, which she'd taken to spoiling whenever she visited her sister.

"I know you like hard rock," he said, pouring a generous amount of syrup over his pancakes.

She salted and peppered her eggs, then mixed them with her hash browns. "My tastes vary," she admitted. She liked everything from hard rock to hip-hop to the stuff from the sixties and seventies her mother used to play so often, in addition to classical and opera. In fact, she was supposed to accompany her grandmother to a chamber music performance Sunday afternoon. "Let me guess, you're a country boy at heart."

He shook his head and his grin turned sheepish. "Motown. None of those CD remakes or compilations, either. Vinyl or nothing at all."

She'd like to see him in nothing at all. "Temptations or Four Tops?" she asked, reining in those baser thoughts that could lead her straight to a broken heart.

"Temptations. Especially the earlier stuff before they cut David Ruffin loose." He cut into a sausage link, then dragged it through the syrup pooling on his plate. "And before you ask, Smokey Robinson is a songwriting genius."

"If we're talking old school, I prefer Lennon and McCartney. Or Elton John and Bernie Taupin. But a man who knows his Motown…?" She plucked a strip of bacon from her plate. "Impressive. So what brings you to Boston, Sebastian? Escaping an ex-wife? Girlfriend, maybe?"

His crooked smile had her pulse thumping pleasantly. Among other, more intimate places.

"Is that your way of wanting to know if I'm single?"

She took a bite of her bacon, smiled and nodded.

"Single. Never been married. You?"

"Same," she said. Although, she'd been close once. Dangerously so. Two and a half years ago she'd been twenty-four hours away from walking down the aisle at the perfect society wedding when she'd discovered her fiancé hadn't stopped dating. The jerk.

"And you're in Boston because…?"

"Work," he said, cutting into his pancakes.

"Work? What kind of work?"

"I'm a lawyer."

She couldn't help herself. She laughed.

He smiled. "Don't start," he said, his tone laced with humor. "There probably isn't a lawyer joke I haven't heard."

"It's not that," she said, then burst out laughing again. So much for her wanting to be *just Joey* tonight. Well, she thought, at least he'd understand the demands of her job. Not that it really made any difference. Beyond tonight, anyway.

"What's so funny?"

"I'm a lawyer," she admitted. "A litigator, actually."

His smile slowly faded. "Yeah?"

Uh-oh. So much for all those intriguing possibilities. She wondered how long it'd take him to get to the door.

"What firm?"

Her own smile waned and she frowned. Wait a minute. Didn't he say he was from Miami? Wasn't the new head of…

Oh no. It couldn't be the same…it just couldn't be *him.*

This was more than a coincidence, it was *insane.* And unfair! The first time in months she'd actually been attracted to a man and he was off-limits? So totally not fair!

"Samuel, Cyrus and Kane," she said.

He pushed his plate aside as if he'd just lost his

appetite. She could relate. Hers had already evaporated.

Over the table, he thrust his hand toward her, which she automatically took. "Sebastian Stanhope," he said, and gave her hand a brisk, impersonal shake. "Samuel, Cyrus and Kane's new—"

"Head of litigation," she finished, and dropped his hand. "And my new boss."

3

"DID YOU SAY BOSS?"

Joey reached for her leather jacket and jammed her hand into the pocket for the small wad of bills. "That I did." She peeled off a twenty and dropped it on the table. "It's been a pleasure, Mr. Stanhope. See you Monday."

She scooted from the booth, her movements jerky as she shrugged into her jacket. A mixture of disappointment and deep frustration, which she couldn't entirely discount as sexual in nature, collided inside her.

"Joey, wait."

"Some other time," she said, knowing it was a lie. Then she hightailed it out the front door.

A blast of cold January air bit at her exposed skin and whipped her hair into her face. A bone-deep chill instantly settled over her. Shivering, she shoved her hair from her face before tugging up the collar of her jacket, looking for warmth. With her hands tucked inside her pockets, she hunkered down and hurried to her car, which was sitting across the street at Rosalie's.

The lot was deserted with the exception of her sporty red BMW parked under the hazy glow of a security light. A silver SUV with a Florida license plate sat a few yards away. Stanhope's.

Still shivering, she pulled out her keys and pressed the button for the keyless entry to unlock her car. Just her rotten luck. Finally, she meets a guy who doesn't have jerkwad written all over him, one who would actually understand the concept of billable hours and the demands of being a career-hungry associate attorney in a large firm, and he was as off-limits as they came. No way could she allow anything interesting to happen now—not with the revelation of Sebastian Stanhope being her new boss.

"Shit," she muttered and yanked open the door. She climbed into the driver's seat and fired the engine before tugging the door closed with a hard slam. And things had been going so well, too, she thought. Well enough that she'd been seriously considering that a brief affair might not be such a bad idea after all.

She cranked up the heater and sat trembling in the cold, cursing and giving the engine time to warm. Sometimes, life just wasn't fair. Maybe she should've gone to Chassy tonight and hung out with her half sister, after all. But no, tonight she'd wanted to be just Joey and what had it gotten her? A whole lot of nothing except an ache between her legs she so wanted Sebastian to ease.

His shadow, cast from the light above, appeared seconds before she heard his gentle rap against the driver's side window. For the space of a heartbeat she considered telling him to get lost. Instead she hefted a weighty sigh and motioned for him to join her inside the slowly growing warmth of her car.

He opened the door and slid that long, gorgeous body into the passenger seat beside her. The luscious scent of him did crazy things to her senses…like obliterate every last one of them.

"Was it something I said?"

"Yeah," she answered and looked over at him. Her stomach took a tumble at the crooked smile curving that very kissable mouth. There should be a law in the books somewhere declaring it illegal for a man to be so incredibly sexy when he was seriously off-limits. "Samuel, Cyrus and Kane."

"Look, I didn't know." Regret tinged his deep, velvety voice. "I *am* sorry."

So was she. More than he realized. And a hell of a lot more than she'd expected, for that matter. "It's just one of those weird coincidences," she said with a shrug. "No need to apologize."

Most of the time, she was a realist. And the reality of the situation was that she was wildly attracted to Sebastian Stanhope, even though he practically came with a "do not touch" brand burned into what she'd been fantasizing were hard, lean abs.

She muttered another curse.

"Would it help if I said I wish things had turned out differently?" he asked.

The sincerity in his eyes irritated her. God, why couldn't he have been a jerk? Then she wouldn't give a rat's ass that her sexual fantasies had come to a screeching halt. Of course, that was her problem, wasn't it? Because she couldn't stop imagining him hot and hard and naked.

"Not really," she countered dryly.

A full smile curved his lips now. "I'll take that as a compliment."

She narrowed her gaze. "Don't tease me, Stanhope. I'm a frustrated woman. That makes me dangerous and highly irrational."

He had the audacity to chuckle. "I like you, Joey."

Yeah, well, the feeling was definitely mutual. "Guess that'll make for a good working relationship, now, won't it?"

She slumped down in her seat. What was she

saying? Working with him would be nothing short of torture. Long hours. Late nights. That incredible scent of his lingering in her office long after he'd gone, driving her to distraction. Those intoxicating eyes.

Oh, God. She was toast. A walking hormonal disaster. A ticking sexual time bomb. It wouldn't take much for him to light her fuse, either. And he was just arrogant enough to realize it, too.

She looked over at him. "Too bad Rosalie's is closed. I could use a drink."

"Yeah, me, too."

At least he agreed with her. That was something, right? Not that they could do anything about it. Dammit.

He tugged his key ring from his pocket and aimed the big black key at the Jeep Commander. He pressed the button and electronically started the vehicle.

Or could they?

Pulling herself up, she smiled at him. "You know, Sebastian, you really *aren't* my boss—" she glanced at the digital display on the Beemer's stereo system "—for another fifty-five hours."

He made a sound that could've been a laugh. Or maybe a short bark of surprise. She couldn't be sure. The smile on his handsome face had faded. Too bad. Feminine instinct told her they could've made good use of those hours.

"You realize we're a sexual harassment claim waiting to happen."

"Not for another fifty-five hours," she argued.

"But what about intent?"

A weak legal argument if she ever heard one. "Are you questioning my intentions, counselor?" she asked, her tone going all husky.

In the soft glow of the dashboard lights, his eyes darkened. "Should I?"

She settled her hand on his arm. "It would be in your best interest. Yes."

The air around them sizzled, crackling with energy. His gaze dipped to her mouth, then he shifted in the seat next to her. That he wasn't immune to her spoke volumes, at least on her radar.

Life was filled with choices. Good ones, and not-so-good ones. Then there were the plain stupid ones. She wasn't exactly certain where she'd classify coming on to Sebastian after his disappointing revelation. Come Monday morning, plain stupid would most assuredly apply.

But it wasn't Monday morning. Yet.

"You're a difficult woman to resist," he said.

She didn't detect so much as an ounce of regret in his admission. So did that mean he was buying her paper-thin argument? Oh, but she hoped so.

She gave his arm a gentle squeeze. "Then don't."

He blew out a stream of breath. "You realize we're on the verge of complicating our professional relationship."

"Probably," she admitted. "But we won't have a professional relationship for—"

He smiled again. "Yes, I know. For another fifty-five hours."

"Exactly."

He pulled his arm from her grasp, but grabbed hold of her hand and laced their fingers together. Her heart rate took off like a rocket when he brought their joined hands to his mouth. His lips brushed lightly over her knuckles and she forgot to breathe.

"Your argument *is* weak." Turning her wrist, he lightly pressed his lips against her rapidly beating pulse. Heat shot through her and settled low in her tummy.

The first genuine tug of desire pulled at her. "So is my willpower," she said, her voice a strained, breathless whisper.

He shifted in his seat and reached for her, sliding his fingers behind her neck and gently pulling her toward him. "I think I left mine in Miami."

Thank God.

His lips brushed hers in a feathery kiss, but it was nowhere near enough. She leaned into him, as far as the bucket seat would allow, and opened her mouth beneath his. His answering groan as he slipped his tongue into her mouth was all the encouragement she needed.

Heat pooled in her belly, filling her with languid warmth. Was it so wrong to have what promised to be a very satisfying one-night stand? They were mature adults. Consenting adults. Why the hell not?

Okay, sure. So maybe he did have a point. They could very well end up complicating their professional relationship, but professional was the only *relationship* they would ever have as far as she was concerned.

He kissed her slow and deep, snapping that final thread of common sense she'd managed to hang on to thus far. A one-night stand was hardly happily-ever-after. She wasn't even looking at a short-term fling beyond tonight. Heaven forbid they should embark upon a torrid office romance. Those always ended badly, anyway. Usually with someone in tears. And she'd bet her overinflated trust fund, Sebastian wouldn't be the one reaching for the tissues.

Using his thumbs, he tipped her head back as his mouth left hers to nuzzle her throat. The delightful little dance his tongue made against her heated flesh was almost too much for her to bear. She wanted more. And she wanted it now.

Inviting him back to her place was out of the question, but…

"Sebastian," she breathed, "let's go where we can be more comfortable."

He lifted his head, but kept his hand cupping her neck. His thumb drew lazy circles along her jaw and she trembled. "Are you sure?"

"I've never been more sure of anything in my life."

"Okay, but just for a nightcap."

Sure, she believed that. *Not.*

"By the way," she said, giving him a sly, but deliberate smile. "Did I mention the beachfront property I have for sale in Arizona?"

IN THE DARKNESS OF his newly rented third-floor apartment, they tripped over a moving carton partially blocking the doorway to his bedroom. Sebastian cursed and Joey giggled, but he caught them both before they went tumbling and landed on the hardwood floor. His place was hardly the ideal scene for romance with a beautiful woman, but when Joey had insisted her place was too far away from Rosalie's to be the practical choice, he hadn't had enough sense left to argue with her.

They landed up against the door with a loud thud. He caught her weight with his body, but the door swung hard against the wall, then jerked again, slamming the knob through the drywall. With Joey's slender curves pressed against him, he didn't much care if the damn thing came off the hinges.

Joey tugged his shirt from his jeans and shoved her hands beneath the fabric to splay her hands over his stomach. Her fingertips teased the waistband of his jeans.

"Your skin is so warm," she murmured. She shoved the shirt up and placed her wet, moist lips on his chest. "Hot."

His skin wasn't all that was on fire. His dick throbbed almost painfully within the strict confines of his jeans. He couldn't remember the last time a woman had him so hard—and all they'd done so far was kiss. Hell, he couldn't remember the last time he'd let his guard down long enough to just be himself with any woman. All work and no play. His own personal motto, one he'd chosen to ignore for the first time in what suddenly felt like an eternity.

She smoothed her hands upward, brushing her palms over his nipples. A rush of breath left him, and he grabbed hold of her hips, pulling her tighter against him. The door creaked, protesting against their weight, but he was beyond caring about anything except having Joey naked and wanting him.

He dove a hand into her short blond hair and tugged gently, pulling her head back so he could kiss her again. She opened for him, inviting him inside. Her taste was sweet and wildly exotic, like a fine brandy. The kind he'd promised himself he'd one day be able to afford.

That thought nearly had him calling a halt to their nocturnal activities…until she arched her body, rubbing her slender curves up against him like a cat.

"Touch me," she murmured against his mouth. "Touch me now, Sebastian."

"Where would you like me to start?" He had a few ideas of his own, but he liked a woman who knew what she wanted and wasn't shy about telling him.

"How about I let you decide?"

He wasn't picky. He liked the sound of that, too.

She backed away, and he instantly regretted the loss of her body heat. In the moonlight streaming through the window, he watched her smile turn positively wicked as she shrugged out of her suede jacket. The heavy material landed on the floor at his feet.

He took a step toward her, but she backed up, keeping him a fraction beyond arm's length away. This time she peeled off her blouse, slowly revealing inch after delicious inch of silky-looking skin. The top went somewhere—to the floor, he assumed—but he didn't happen to notice where because his gaze was held prisoner by the sight of a red satin-and-lace bra cupping her firm, lush breasts.

His fingers itched to fulfill her demand to touch her, to test the weight of her full breasts in his hands. He wanted to taste her skin, longed to discover her secrets. Couldn't wait to make her his in the most elemental way possible. For as long as it lasted, which according to her, would only be until they reported for work Monday morning.

With a flick of her wrist, she unbuttoned her jeans then slowly tugged the zipper down. He caught a glimpse of more red lace. Thong, he wondered? Or a sexy pair of those boy shorts he easily imagined hugging that adorable ass of hers?

A frown suddenly puckered her smooth forehead. "Boots," she said, then plopped down on the edge of the bed.

"Here." He bent and lifted her foot, resting it on his thigh. "Let me."

Gently, he tugged the boot from one foot, then the other. The leather was supple and expensive, as he'd suspected earlier. His curiosity about her climbed another notch. She hustled pool, yet drove a BMW he doubted was more than a year old, yet she was only a junior associate. He'd lived the pay scale, and while he'd had no trouble making ends meet, no way could he have afforded anything as slick as Joey's Beemer. His ten-year-old Honda Civic had been on its last leg when he'd bought the Jeep Commander, and he'd only been able to afford that with the bonus the partners had paid him after he'd won a multimillion-dollar products liability case.

Joey was full of secrets. Too bad he didn't have time to unravel more of her mysteries.

Before she could object or slip away, he took advantage of her position on the bed and leaned in, urging her back on the mattress. He slid his hands to her waist and hooked his fingers into the waistband. She lifted her hips and he slowly eased her jeans down her legs, and smiled. "Boy shorts."

"I've shown you mine," she said with a teasing smile on her lips. "Now show me yours."

He yanked off his shirt and tossed it aside. "I suppose it's only fair." He moved to join her on the bed.

She held up her hand to stop him. "Uh-uh, counselor. Not so fast." She reached for the waistband of his jeans and easily popped the button. "Full disclosure."

He toed off his shoes and kicked them aside, then shrugged out of his jeans. His boxer briefs were next.

Acute awareness powered Joey's senses as she looked her fill of Sebastian's powerful, athletic body. The man was nothing short of a work of art.

The dullness of winter faded and the dark colors seemingly turned brighter, as if springtime had entered the sparse bedroom with them. She was assaulted with a delicious vibrancy to her senses. The warmth of Sebastian's skin as he joined her on the bed. The tickle of soft chest hair against her breasts as he leaned over her. The heat of his body as he kissed her deeply, thoroughly.

She felt as if she'd been struck by a bolt of lightning. A rushing surge of intensity increased the sexual energy that had been haunting them since he'd approached her at the jukebox.

His lips and tongue tasted sweet, like the wine they'd shared from a single paper cup upon arriving at his apartment, until his mouth became hotter and more demanding as his tongue mated with hers. The gentle glide of his hands as he swept them over her breasts turned into an insistent quest to bring them both pleasure.

The need to touch him, to fully explore the tempting landscape, drove her. She smoothed her palm over his belly, loving the way the taut muscle danced in response to her touch. His low moan of pleasure encouraged her to continue her exploration. She slid her hand lower and sifted her way through the rough furring of curls to slide her fingers over his long, hard length.

Her blood fired and a hushed gasp of delight escaped her at the feel of him hot and heavy and pulsing in her hand. Oh how she wanted him inside her, but it was too soon. She summoned her patience because she knew without a doubt, she'd be rewarded.

Breaking the kiss, he reached for her hand and held it above her head on the bed. She murmured a protest, but he merely chuckled, then nipped and soothed, tasted and laved a fiery path to her breasts. His mouth settled over her nipple through the lace of her bra, sending a spiral of heat shooting through her veins like wildfire.

He released her hand and with a move she hadn't even seen coming, freed her breasts from her bra. Her breath quickened when he took her nipple fully into the heat of his mouth and sucked.

Sparks of pleasure assailed her and she let out a low purr of encouragement as he wound a path with his tongue down her torso. She felt the press of his fingers in the waistband of her panties, his fingertips teasing her by dipping beneath the lacy edge.

"I want to taste you."

His hot breath against her tummy drove her crazy. The tips of his fingers teased her moist curls, drawing closer to where she wanted him to touch her the most, making her nuts. She rolled her hips in response, because if he didn't fulfill his promise, if she didn't feel the heat of his mouth against her sex soon, she'd surely go certifiably insane.

He rolled her panties past her hips and down her legs.

"Open for me, Joey," he whispered, then placed a kiss just below her belly button.

An elusive sensation she couldn't name curled inside her. She didn't think, doubted she could muster more than a fleeting thought, as the anticipation heightened. She merely obeyed and opened her legs for him.

He settled to his knees on the floor and carefully scooted her to the edge of the bed. He pressed her thighs even wider, opening her to him completely.

He lightly brushed his knuckles over her folds. "Hmmm," he murmured softly. He circled her opening with the tip of his finger. "So wet."

Her breath momentarily stilled at the awe in his voice. Desire burned volcanic hot, making her a willing casualty to his demand for control.

She wasn't accustomed to being so exposed, regardless of the situation. In her world, she was the one in control. Always. Sebastian obviously had other plans.

She felt that mysterious sensation curling inside her again, but before she could name it, she felt the first feathery brush of his tongue against her sex. Her heart nearly stopped beating. When he gently suckled her clit, and his fingers dipped inside her, gently thrusting and withdrawing, she knew she'd just died and landed right into heaven.

The intensity of the pressure building inside her was nothing short of exquisite torture. Little else mattered except the moist warmth of his mouth and fingers making love to her, pushing her that much closer to what promised to be a mind-blowing orgasm.

He grazed her clit with his teeth and her body tensed from the intensity of sensations. She closed her eyes and the world exploded. Blood pounded in her ears and rushed through her veins. Nothing mattered except the primal need for satisfaction.

Sebastian struggled to rein in the need clawing at his belly with knife-like sharpness at the sexy sound of Joey's cries of pleasure. He wanted to be inside her, to feel her body tense and clench when she came.

Without giving her a chance to cool, he reached for the bedside table and snagged a condom from the drawer. He quickly sheathed himself, then moved them to the center of the bed.

She welcomed him inside her, lifting her hips to meet his initial thrust. Coherent thought escaped him. His concentration centered on the ebb and flow of their bodies coming together in an explosion of heat and fulfillment.

There was nothing gentle or slow about the way they made love. She met him, thrust for thrust. Her breath came in short, hard pants. He struggled for his own breath when her body tightened around his thick shaft as another orgasm rocked her body.

He felt wild and primal as he stroked her body with his. He drove into her again and again. Deeper. Harder. Tension climbed. His body burned from the strain of muscle as he lost himself in the power of his own release.

Eventually his senses began a slow return. The first thing he became aware of was the leisurely sensation of her fingertips gliding lightly over his back. He moved off her, but pulled her close and dragged the bedclothes over their cooling bodies.

She snuggled closer and he draped his leg over her hers. With her head nestled in the crook of his arm, he closed his eyes and breathed in the sweet, musky scent of their lovemaking.

"Joey?"

"Hmm?" she murmured drowsily. She wiggled closer, her backside rubbing enticingly against his groin.

"I think it's safe to say we just trashed our professional relationship."

4

JOEY ZIPPED UP her jeans and winced, certain the sound echoed so loudly throughout the sparsely furnished room it could be heard in the next apartment. She knew she was being silly, but she was hoping to escape without waking Sebastian. Or more honestly, hoping to avoid an awkward situation.

Only hours ago, just before she'd eventually fallen asleep sprawled across Sebastian's chest, the pinkish gray fingers of dawn had been creeping across the city's winter skyline. Without a clock handy, she'd guessed the hour now to be somewhere in the vicinity of noon. She snagged her watch from the nightstand for confirmation. Twelve-twenty.

God, why had she slept with him? Not that she hadn't enjoyed every perfect second, but that was beside the point. In two days she'd have to face him again, fully clothed this time, and she had every intention of pretending last night never happened. A feat she imagined would be next to impossible. Especially now. They'd made love again and again, taking their time to fully explore each other's bodies. It'd been beautiful, sweet, and had caused something to stir deep inside her—something other than her libido.

Oh, yeah. She was so out of there, if only to distance herself from the memory of their lovemaking and that strange little flutter she couldn't, or wouldn't, explain.

She crept around the bed in search of her bra and found it dangling from the edge of a tall moving carton near the closet. After slipping into it, she scooped up her top a few feet away and pulled it on as well. Her boots lay on the floor near Sebastian's side of the bed. As quietly as possible, she stooped to pick them up, but couldn't find her socks.

Full sunlight streamed through the windows, which made it easy for her to see them peeking out from under the bed, but she practically had to crawl beneath it to snag them. Her breathing stilled when she heard Sebastian stir.

Please don't wake up.

Slowly, she lifted her head, peeked over the edge of the mattress and let out a startled gasp. Sebastian lay on his side, his head propped in his hand, staring down at her…and wearing nothing but a lazy smile.

Damn. So much for escaping unnoticed.

"Going somewhere?" he asked, his voice thick from sleep.

"I didn't want to disturb you."

He chuckled. "Sure you didn't." His thick hair was mussed and his smile went from lazy to cocky. The man looked way too sexy and far too tempting for a woman filled with morning-after regret.

"Um…I have to water my plants." The excuse was beyond lame, and from the skeptical light that entered those dark, bedroom eyes, they both knew it. But dammit, he seriously rocked her composure. What did he expect? A Rhodes scholar?

She dropped onto the edge of the bed to slip on her socks. He shifted beside her and brought his body closer to hers. Warning bells went off in her head. Lordy, but the temptation to crawl beneath the covers with him again was tough to resist.

He smoothed his hand down her back. She thought about the pleasure those hands could bring her and her resolve nearly crumbled.

She stiffened her spine.

"We have a problem, Joey."

"Great deduction, Watson."

He ignored her sass. "I want to see you again."

A different kind of regret filled her. In all honesty, she'd love nothing more than to spend more time with Sebastian, in and out of bed, but it was out of the question. Forget that he was technically her supervisor, he was smart, sexy and dangerous. The kind of guy that could easily break her heart. The kind she could easily fall for…hard.

She shoved her foot into her boot and tugged. "Sorry," she said with a shrug as she glanced down at him. "It's pumpkin time, Cinderella."

He frowned. "It's only Saturday."

"Can't," she said brusquely, then pulled on her other boot. "I'm busy."

She wasn't. She had no plans whatsoever until tomorrow afternoon, but he didn't need to know that. Although Molly would more than likely have worked herself into a feline snit by the time she did get home. Her persnickety cat didn't appreciate being left to her own devices all night and half the day, but a treat and some cuddle time would smooth her leopardlike fur to some degree.

She cast a quick glance in his direction. If his narrow-eyed stare was any indication, he wasn't buying her line of BS. Too bad. She needed time to distance herself from him, to regain her composure before she faced him in the office Monday morning.

Good luck.

She let out a sigh and stood. "I think it's best if we just pretend last night never happened." She located her leather jacket near the bedroom door and shrugged into it.

He swung his feet to the floor and came off the bed in one easy movement. Heaven help her, she stared. She just couldn't help herself. In the light of day, Sebastian Stanhope was even more glorious.

The erection he was sporting wasn't half-bad, either.

Heat rushed to her face and she lifted her gaze to his. "I had a lovely time," she said in a nervous rush, "but I really do have to go home." *To take a cold shower.*

Her throat constricted when he crossed the room. Those pleasure-giving hands settled on her upper arms, sending tiny tremors of delight chasing over her skin.

"Stay with me today."

She bit her lip. The man was temptation personified. And trouble, with a big fat *T.*

She shook her head and looked away. "I can't," she said, hating that she had no choice but to deny him. Hating even more the regret so blatantly evident in her voice.

He tucked his fingers under her chin and gently turned her to face him. "Another time, another place?"

No truer words, she thought sadly. "Yeah," she whispered in agreement. "Another time."

He dipped his head and kissed her. Deeply, tenderly. Fool that she was, she kissed him back, enjoying this last parting moment even though her heart suddenly ached. Because there'd be no more kisses for them? Ever? Or because she'd already started falling for him?

She refused to even consider the answer. Regretfully, she ended the kiss. "Goodbye, Sebastian."

She spun on her heel and left. By the time she hit the pavement, her hopes that the next two days would be long enough for her to convince herself that making love to Sebastian hadn't been a monumental and earth-shattering experience were practically nonexistent.

"WHERE HAVE YOU BEEN? I've been calling you all morning."

Joey didn't appreciate the accusation in Brooke's tone, but figured it was her guilty conscience making her feel mildly agitated. "I turned off my cell."

"Since when don't you check for messages?"

"Gee," she said, standing back to let her older sister inside the small foyer of the carriage house, "nice to see you, too."

Brooke set a large shopping bag with the Worthington logo on the front on the antique bench. She worked at the department store as a window dresser.

"These are for Reba," she said, unwinding a wool scarf from her neck. "I thought she might like them."

Joey peered into the bag, but the clothing items were all carefully wrapped in delicate tissue paper. That was so Brooke, she thought. "Didn't we go through all of Mom's things a couple of months ago?"

"We did." Brooke hung her scarf on the hook by the door, then shrugged out of her wool coat. "I found those in the back of Mom's closet."

"And you brought them here because…?"

"Because you said you were taking Reba to lunch next week."

Since their mother's passing, she, Brooke and Katie had taken to looking in on Reba, their mother's oldest and closest friend. Joey managed a weak smile. "Ah, yes," she murmured. She'd forgotten, primarily because her mind had been elsewhere. Like on Sebastian.

"I was about to make some tea. Want some?"

Brooke rubbed her hands over her upper arms. "Perfect. It's freezing out there today."

"Amazing how that happens every January." Joey flashed her sister a saucy grin, then took off for the kitchen. She had the kettle filled and on the stove by the time Brooke joined her.

Joey reached into the cabinet for a teak serving tray, then carefully brought down a pair of delicate china cups and the matching teapot. "Are you coming to dinner next week?"

Brooke shrugged and looked away. "I'm not sure."

Joey let out a sigh, although she understood her sister's reluctance to walk inside the lion's den. "The Admiral keeps asking about you."

Ever since Brooke had dropped the bomb on her grandparents that she wasn't a Winfield by birth, her relationship with their grandmother had been strained at best. Joey suspected the tension in their relationship stemmed not so much because of Brooke's parentage, but because of the scandalous photos of a topless Brooke and Boston's bad boy, David Carrera, that had shown up in the tabloids. Heaven forbid a Winfield should cause tongues to wag.

"I'll think about it," Brooke said, but Joey doubted the subject was usually far from Brooke's mind. Familial duty had always been high on her elder sister's list of priorities.

Brooke crossed her arms and leaned back against the ceramic-tiled counter. "So, where were you?"

It was Joey's turn to shrug. "Nowhere important." She aimed for nonchalance but ended up closer to high-pitched and guilt-ridden. What was she supposed to say? That she'd spent the night boffing her new boss's brains out? And enjoying every glorious second of it?

She added tea leaves to the strainer before sliding a quick glance in Brooke's direction. Her sister gave her one of those looks, the kind only an older sister had the secret password to. The kind that said she knew Joey was full of crap.

Brooke offered one of her more irritating smiles. "So? Who is he?"

Joey concentrated on cutting into the leftover crumb coffee cake she'd pilfered from her grandmother's cook. "It really doesn't matter."

"Are you going to see him again?"

"That all depends on how you might define 'seeing him again,'" Joey answered cryptically. Technically, she'd be spending a great deal of time with Sebastian, but not in the way Brooke meant.

The teakettle started to whistle. "Saved by the whistle."

"Bell," Brooke corrected.

"Whatever. A distraction is a distraction as far as I'm concerned. I'll take what I can get."

"You're not getting off that easy," Brooke said with a laugh as Joey poured the steaming water into the teapot. "Now I really want details. Who is this guy?"

She refused to make a big deal out of her one-time-only, never-gonna-happen-again night of sexual bliss with Sebastian. What was the point?

"Joey?"

Joey popped the crumb cake slices into the microwave and pressed the reheat button. "You're not going to let up until I tell you, are you?"

Brooke's irritating smile widened. "Nope."

The microwave dinged. Joey arranged the dessert plates on the tray along with the items for tea.

"He's my boss," she said in a rush. She picked up the tray and hurried into the cozy living room, as if that would be the end of the conversation. With her sisters, not gonna happen.

A fire burned in the stone fireplace. Molly lay curled on the arm of the chintz chair near the leaded glass window overlooking the winter dormant garden.

Brooke joined her, concern evident in her soft brown eyes. "Define 'boss.'"

"Oh, no, not any of *them*." Joey shuddered, knowing Brooke was thinking of one of the three middle-aged senior partners of the firm. "The new guy they hired to head up the litigation division." Last night when she'd met her sisters for dinner, she'd mentioned the new guy the partners had recruited from a Miami firm, and how she'd been relegated to second chair in *Gilson v. Pierce*. One thing sleeping with Sebastian hadn't changed—her disappointment and irritation over having the lead counsel position on the *Gilson* matter taken away from her.

Joey shooed Molly from the chair, while Brooke

poured tea. "My *new* boss," she admitted, taking the teacup Brooke held out for her. "Sebastian Stanhope."

"Stanhope?" At Joey's nod, Brooke asked, "Is he any relation to Emerson Stanhope?"

The Stanhopes were one of Boston's oldest and most prominent families. In fact she was fairly certain Emerson and her father had once had some sort of business dealings. "Uh…" Joey hedged, "I don't know. That's a subject that never came up."

Brooke set her cup on the table. "Joey—"

"Don't say it." Joey dropped a sugar cube into her cup and stirred. "It was a one-time thing and trust me, one that won't be happening again."

"Did you know who he was before you slept with him?" Brooke asked, adding a splash of cream to her Earl Grey.

Joey scrunched up her nose and nodded. "Not one of my smarter decisions." But one she wouldn't apologize for, either. Regardless of the ethics involved, and no matter how plain stupid her choice had been, she simply could not regret making love to Sebastian. Not completely.

"Joey, how did this happen?" There was no accusation or even judgment in Brooke's tone, only concern.

Joey leaned back and pulled her feet up onto the chair. She recounted how she'd gone to Rosalie's last night and had been rendered temporarily insane by the instantaneous attraction between her and Sebastian. When she finished, she set her empty teacup on the rosewood side table and let out a sigh. "I plead hormones," she said. "It's a valid affirmative defense."

"I doubt that." Brooke tapped her fingernail against the side of her cup. "So what happens now?"

"Nothing," Joey said adamantly. Molly hopped into her lap and rubbed her head against Joey's hand, demanding affection. She smoothed her hand over the cat's thick fur. "Monday morning I go into the office and pretend Friday night never happened."

"For your sake," Brooke said, "I really do hope you know what you're doing."

"I do," Joey said firmly. She dropped her head against the back of the chair, hoping she was right.

"So how does it feel being back in the old neighborhood?" Hunter McAllister asked around a mouthful of pepperoni pizza.

Sebastian twisted the cap off the bottle of beer and chucked it halfway across the living room into the cardboard box pulling temporary duty as a trash bin. "Cold," he said to his childhood friend. "I'd forgotten how freaking cold it can get up here."

He didn't bother to remind Hunter that the revitalized North End of Boston was hardly the rough South Boston neighborhood where they'd spent their youth. Even though Sebastian had decided to live in the North End, in his heart, they would always be Southies.

Hunter balanced his beer bottle on his knee. "Why you'd give up year-round bathing beauties for Beacon Hill snobs is beyond me."

"Right," Sebastian said. "If a woman has a pulse, you're interested."

"Hey, is it my fault women have a thing for a man in uniform?"

Sebastian seriously doubted Hunter's Boston P.D. uniform had anything to do with it. His friend had been a chick magnet for as long as Sebastian could remember.

"Personally," Hunter said, swiping the last slice of pizza, "I don't think mystery and that whole 'more is less' crap is what it's cracked up to be. Gimme skin any day. And lots of it. And you willingly walk away from it to come back here? Dude, you need your head examined."

If Hunter knew how little time Sebastian had actually spent on the beaches of Miami or enjoying the bathing beauties, as his friend referred to the bikini-clad set, he'd be drummed out of the corps for life. Work hard and then work even harder. Truth be told, Friday night's encounter with Joey was the most fun he'd had with the opposite sex in too damn long.

Too bad that one night was all he'd have, even if it never should've happened. He was no stranger to one-night stands, not that he made a habit of them. But tangling the sheets with a woman he'd known upfront he'd be not only working with but supervising, had been a mistake of the first order. Yet even that knowledge did little to stop the pang of disappointment he'd felt yesterday morning when Joey had declined his offer to spend the day together.

At least one of them had been thinking clearly, he thought. He'd been thinking, too, but not with the head above his shoulders.

He'd made good use of the time alone and had kept busy, even if thoughts of Joey had derailed his concentration and good intentions several times throughout the day. Most of the shipping cartons had been unpacked and he'd managed to put his apartment in pretty good shape. And like a good son, he'd even taken the time last night to take his mom to dinner.

Yet despite his good intentions and the distraction Hunter had provided today with pizza, beer and NFL wild card games on the tube, his thoughts continued to stray to Joey. The sparkling shade of blue her eyes turned when she was aroused. The way her hair brushed against his abdomen like a cloud of silk when she'd loved him with her mouth.

He blew out a ragged stream of breath. He needed to get a grip. Or a life.

"Mystery has it perks," he said suddenly. Discovering a woman's secrets—Joey's in particular.

"What?" Hunter asked, his attention back on the game.

"Women." Sebastian took a swig of beer. "The feminine mystique. It's not so bad."

Hunter frowned and shot him a glance. "What the hell are you talking about?"

Sebastian shook his head. "Forget it." He picked up the empty pizza box and walked into the kitchen, stopping midway to watch the Pittsburgh Steelers' quarterback throw his second interception of the quarter.

"Bench him," Hunter bellowed at the television set. "That kid just can't handle pressure. We're gonna cream them next week, provided Pitt can pull this one out of their asses to even get there."

By "we," Sebastian knew Hunter meant the New England Patriots. "He's still young," Sebastian said, defending the quarterback. "Cut him some slack."

The partners wouldn't be cutting him any slack if they found out that he'd slept with one of their associates. There'd been no excuse for it. He'd known better, yet he'd ignored his instincts and charged full bore into the danger zone with a woman whose last name he didn't even know. If anyone found out what he'd done, he'd be benched right out of a job.

He supposed there was a bright side. Joey had made it clear she didn't seem all that inclined to pursue a relationship outside of the office. For reasons he didn't care to examine too carefully, that thought irritated the hell out of him.

5

UNLIKE MOST OF the associate attorneys at the firm who would've been in their offices no later than seven-thirty already racking up billable hours, Joey had been sitting impatiently in a courtroom waiting for Ginny Karnes to be arraigned. Under normal circumstances, she might have been antsy to get into the office herself. Except today was Sebastian's first day at Samuel, Cyrus and Kane and she was grateful for the brief reprieve, glad to have a legitimate excuse to avoid "meeting" her new boss for as long as possible.

Why, oh, why had she slept with him?

The answer was painfully obvious—because she couldn't help herself. She'd wanted him and she'd listened to her inner bad girl…again. There was something seriously tweaked with her DNA. All of her sisters possessed their mother's minor rebellious streak, but she'd inherited more than her fair share—all the way to the nth degree.

Cold air blasted her as she left the courthouse, so she burrowed deeper into her black wool coat. No one had to know she'd slept with Sebastian. All she had to do was play it cool and no one would ever guess she had a serious case of lust going for the firm's newest hotshot. More importantly, no one would ever know she hadn't been able to stop thinking about the man all weekend long, either. Especially not him, the object of her obsession…er…thoughts.

The sprinkling of snow dusting the sidewalks swirled around Joey's feet as she made her way to the office a few blocks away. The early morning snowfall was only a precursor to the Nor'easter headed their way. She suspected that by the end of the day traffic out of the city would be nothing short of a nightmare. Another reason she should seriously consider moving out of the carriage house and finding her own place in the city.

Her cell phone rang and she pulled it from her pocket to check the display before answering. "Good morning, Katie," she said to her younger sister.

"Well, how did it go?" Katie asked.

"Better than I'd hoped. My client is being released back to the halfway house later today. Since she'd only been busted with a handful of pre-scription pain relievers, the ADA wasn't interested in revoking her probation."

Katie's impatient sigh was audible. "I meant with Sebastian."

Joey stopped for a red light. She knew exactly what her sister had meant. She let out her own sigh. "Brooke told you."

"Everything," Katie said with a light chuckle. "You didn't think you could keep something like screwing your boss a secret from me, did you?"

"A girl can hope." She was usually much better at keeping her indiscretions private—at least for a little while. She usually ended up confessing to her sisters anyway, but this time she'd been so rattled by her response to Sebastian, she'd spilled her guts to Brooke with very little prodding. Not that she regretted it. She'd needed someone to talk to, but she should've known her secret wouldn't stay that way for long.

Another gust of frigid wind blew through the streets of downtown Boston. Joey shivered and tugged her coat tighter around her. "There's nothing to tell. Yet. I'm headed to the office now."

"Okay, call me later. I want all the juicy details."

"There will be no details, juicy or otherwise."

"Excuse me, but do I have the wrong number? This is Joey, right?"

The light turned green and she stepped off the curb. "I'm hanging up now."

Katie laughed. "Hey, don't forget about Thursday."

"What's Thursday?"

"We're going to Chassy, remember? It's your turn, sister dear."

Joey frowned. A twinge of dread formed in her stomach. "My turn for what?"

Katie let out another impatient sigh. "You're getting your dare this week. Remember?"

That twinge formed into the equivalent of a lead ball, filling her with a sinking feeling. Dare? *Oh, no. Not now.* She had enough on her plate to worry about without having to fulfill some silly dare. Usually she wouldn't hesitate to become a participant, but she'd much rather maintain the status quo and continue as an observer and supporter of the other more daring members of the exclusive women's club.

"I never agreed to that," she argued.

"Yes, you did. Well, sorta."

"I think I said when hell freezes over."

"Just your luck, the weatherman said that'll be most of this week." Laughter tinged Katie's voice. "Anyway, it's all set. Thursday night, seven o'clock sharp. Don't be late."

Before Joey could protest further, Katie hung up. With a curse, Joey flipped her phone closed and tucked it back inside her coat pocket. She'd been so focused on the stupid stunt she'd pulled by sleeping with Sebastian, she'd completely forgotten that she'd offhandedly agreed to officially join Martinis and Bikinis this month.

The M&B meetings held monthly at Chassy, her half sister Lindsay's bar in South Boston, were essentially a women's empowerment and support group. The dares handed out by Lindsay, with a humorous dose of pomp and circumstance, ranged from mild to the more extreme. One member's dare had been nothing more audacious than to put the moves on a sexy new neighbor she'd been lusting over. Brooke's stripping dare last fall had definitely been one of the more extreme, an event which had ended up with a photo of her sister and David splashed across the front page of the local tattler. In Brooke's defense, her sister hadn't really meant to end up doing a topless dance at the strip club. Was it Brooke's fault she didn't realize that pasties required, well, *paste* to stay in place?

The wind kicked up again, harder this time, sending a biting chill through Joey's limbs. She came to a stop for another traffic light and shivered against the biting cold. When the light finally turned green, she rushed across the street, then picked up her pace the rest of the way to the office. Not that she was in a hurry to get there and face Sebastian, but the temperature had dropped a good fifteen degrees during her brief walk from the courthouse. Hell was indeed freezing over.

Another of her not-so-brilliant ideas, she thought as she slipped inside the old brick building. Her toes were frozen and she was convinced the tip of her nose had turned blue. She hadn't thawed a lick, either, by the time she reached Blood Alley.

The firm operated on the top three floors of the twelve-story building. The Dungeon, as it was called—or rather the tenth floor—housed the word processing and accounting departments, along with an impressive law library that took up more than half of the floor. The partners, both junior and senior, were all top-floor execs in what was referred to as the Penthouse, even though it wasn't officially a penthouse suite. The offices were simply gorgeous and worthy of being depicted in *Architectural Digest,* including the four beautifully appointed conference rooms where meetings with important clients and depositions were all held. Her floor, called Blood Alley, was in between the Dungeon and the Penthouse, and was where the real work of the firm was conducted.

She stepped off the elevator and avoided the reception area by heading down the hall past the restroom and the door to the stairwell to the private entrance. With her card key in hand, she zipped it through the security device and slipped through the door.

The area, usually buzzing with the sounds from the various support staff, was deserted with the exception of one of the building's maintenance men. He paid her no attention and was busy using a wireless screwdriver on the door of the office next to hers, which was inhabited by Shelby Martin.

She circled the empty support area and walked toward her office, which was situated between two larger corner offices. The first, belonging to Dillard Bowman, a senior associate and one of the firm's most ambitious litigators, was empty. She peered over the four-foot, mahogany-capped divider to her secretary's desk. Mary had left a file open on her desk and her computer's tropical-fish screen saver showed an array of brilliantly colored fish swimming across the monitor. Since it was only a few minutes after ten, she assumed everyone was in a meeting —one probably called to introduce Sebastian to the litigation division. One to which she was painfully late and no doubt noticeably absent.

Tough, she thought rebelliously. The firm encouraged their associates to partake in pro bono work. The women at the halfway house were important to her, and keeping Ginny Karnes out of jail had been a priority.

Still curious about what the maintenance guy was doing to Shelby's door, she stopped to take a look before entering her small office. She stared, stunned, as he slipped a fresh nameplate into the holder he'd just hung on the door. Her stomach bottomed out. Instead of Shelby Martin, who was one of the more senior litigation associates, the nameplate read Sebastian Stanhope.

Joey stared in disbelief. What was *he* doing *here?* Not just on her floor, but right next to her office? Working with Sebastian would be difficult enough, but she hadn't expected to be working right next to the man.

Her briefcase slipped from her fingers and landed at her feet with a thud. The maintenance guy—Bill, according to the name tag sewn on his blue shirt— turned to look at her. "Can I help you, miss?"

"Surely there's some mistake," she said, inclining her head toward the gold nameplate. "The partners' offices are on the top floor."

Brian Penfield, who ran the bad faith division, wouldn't dream of having his office anywhere near the unwashed masses. Neither would Elizabeth Colton, the stern head of probate and estate planning. For that matter, she was dead positive she'd never even seen Montgomery Kettle, who oversaw the family law division, anywhere near his associates' offices. Wilson Hemmer, one of three partners who headed up the huge corporate-law department, made regular appearances on her floor, as did one of Wilson's counterparts, Illona Goodwin. They'd both been promoted out of the rank and file. Illona had once confided to her after two glasses of wine over dinner that she still felt more comfortable with her "peeps" than on the hallowed ground of the Penthouse.

"This your office?" Bill asked.

Joey shook her head and attempted to summon a smile, but was positive she'd only managed a grimace. "No. Never mind. Sorry to bother you."

She stooped to pick up her briefcase, then entered her small office and closed the door. Why the hell was Sebastian's office on her floor? Not just on her floor, but right next to her? It just wasn't heard of at Samuel, Cyrus and Kane for a partner to have his office on Blood Alley.

She dropped her briefcase on the deep mauve guest chair, then fished her cell phone out of her pocket before hanging her coat on the hook on the back of the door. She thought about calling Brooke, but quickly changed her mind. What would she say; other than whine about the rotten turn of luck she seemed to be having lately? First guy she meets in months that turns her on and he's her new boss. She screws him anyway and now his office is next to hers?

She unwound her Burberry scarf from her neck and slipped it over the hook with her coat, then opened her door. If she kept it closed, would he take the hint and ignore her? For some reason, she seriously doubted it. Closed off wasn't exactly the impression she wanted to give. Besides, if she started closing her door now, wouldn't people wonder about the change? They might even speculate that she resented Sebastian's presence. Well, she did, but not in the way they might construe.

She'd thought about the situation with Sebastian long and hard over the weekend and had decided her best defense would be to play it cool. If she kept a low profile and did what she did best—her job—then no one would ever suspect her of diddling the new guy.

But where had they moved Shelby? And why was Sebastian *here?* She wanted to stomp her foot and whine at the unfairness. She liked having Shelby next door to her. They weren't only work friends, but Shelby Martin had a superb legal mind. Joey enjoyed bouncing ideas around and discussing the latest precedents with her. They'd even graduated from the same law school, although Shelby had graduated eight years before Joey.

She shrugged out of her blazer and carefully folded it over the back of the guest chair, then approached her desk where she found a yellow sticky note posted to the closed lid of her laptop. *West wing. ASAP,* the note said and was signed *M* with a little smiley face. Meaning she was supposed to report to the west conference room upstairs.

She pulled the note from the laptop and tossed it in the trash can under her desk. Might as well get it over with, she thought, as she opened the center drawer and fumbled around for the lipstick she kept there. After applying a little color to her lips, she quickly ran a comb through her wind-tossed hair, straightened her long, red plaid wool skirt and grabbed a fresh legal pad and her favorite pen before leaving her office.

She might as well be facing a firing squad what with the way her insides were jumping. Heaven help her, silly as it was, that's exactly how she felt by the time she reached the Penthouse.

What was her problem? No one knew she'd slept with Sebastian. It wasn't as if she had a scarlet letter sewn to her black silk blouse.

"Good morning, Miss Winfield," the secretary seated behind an elaborately carved mahogany desk said when Joey approached. "They're in the conference room nearest Mr. Kane's office."

"Thank you, Sonja." Joey walked through the waiting room, then headed to the appropriate conference room.

The massive double doors at the end of the western corridor stood open. As she neared, Sebastian's deep, velvety voice washed over her. Addressing the troops, she thought, as she struggled to ignore the delightful little tingle that passed along her skin.

Okay, she thought, slip in quietly and disappear into the crowd. Draw no attention to yourself.

She stopped just outside the door. Sebastian paced a length of gray carpeting directly inside, gesturing in front of everyone seated at the conference table. For courage, she sucked in a deep fortifying breath.

Stepping forward, she wobbled on her heels, then tripped, crashing into the room with all the elegance of an elephant bursting through a china closet.

"ARE YOU ALL RIGHT?" Sebastian asked, helping Joey to her feet. She'd slammed right into him, making a most interesting entrance into the meeting he'd been about to close.

She swept her hands down her skirt, then rubbed at her elbow. "Yes, fine. Thank you." She glanced up at him, a pleading look lighting her gaze. "Sorry to interrupt."

"Good one, Winfield," Dillard Bowman said, causing a few chuckles to circulate around the conference room.

"Just wait until you see what I do for an encore," she quipped.

Damn if she didn't look absolutely adorable, and rattled. "We were just about finished," Sebastian said.

"Would you excuse me, please? I'm late for my class at the local charm school."

More laughter erupted. Sebastian couldn't help himself, he smiled at her. "Why don't you have a seat? I promise to send a note to your teacher explaining why you're late."

"Gee, thanks," she murmured, as she stooped to retrieve a yellow legal pad. She walked to the back of the table and took the only vacant chair.

Sebastian waited until Joey was seated before resuming the meeting. "I'd like to meet with the associates over the next two days to discuss your individual case loads. Laura will be in touch to coordinate meeting times. For now, paralegal and secretarial assignments will remain unchanged. Any questions?"

When none were forthcoming, he added, "That's all for now. Thank you for coming."

He glanced over at Joey, who stood and moved toward the exit. "Joey, would you mind remaining so we can get started now?"

She looked at him sharply. He recognized a deer-in-the-headlights look when he saw one. "I don't have anything prepared." An edge of panic laced her voice.

Her secretary—Mary, he believed her name

was—appeared at Joey's side and slipped her a copy of the case list he'd asked all the secretaries to prepare first thing upon his arrival this morning. He'd wanted to hit the ground running, and the best way to do that was to be briefed on all the open litigation files within his department.

Joey glanced longingly at the exit as she spoke in a hushed tone to her secretary, who jotted notes on a steno pad. Mary said something in return, then left the conference room.

The room slowly emptied, with the exception of his own secretary, Laura. She was a thirtysomething single mom, if the lack of a wedding ring and the framed photos of a pretty little girl with long brown curls on her desk were any indication. "Do you need me to stay?" Laura asked him.

He looked in Joey's direction. "Coffee?"

She shook her head. "No, thank you."

"That'll be all for now," he told Laura. "Thanks."

She offered him a brief smile, then gathered her steno pad and waited for the last few stragglers to depart. "If you need anything, my extension is 427," she said, then left, closing the double doors to the conference room behind her.

Joey smoothed her hands down her skirt again and cleared her throat. "I'm really sorry about that," she said. "My heel must've caught in the floor door lock."

"Don't worry about it," he said, motioning for her to sit. He stilled the provocative and completely inappropriate response hovering on the tip of his tongue—the one about enjoying any excuse to touch her again—and joined her at the far end of the conference table.

"I was wondering if you were going to show up," he said. "I thought maybe you were avoiding me."

She made a sound that resembled a laugh, but wouldn't look at him. "I had an appearance this morning."

"Mary mentioned it was a pro bono matter."

"Yes." She looked at him then, a hard glint entering her gaze. "The senior partners encourage it."

"Joey, I didn't—"

"It's Josephine," she said stiffly. "Or Jo." She glanced pointedly at the list of cases in front of her. "Shall we get started?"

He shook off the sharp stab of disappointment. He didn't know what he was looking for exactly. At the office, he knew business only was the best possible choice. They did both have careers to think about. Besides, he hadn't come this far to throw away everything he'd worked for because he couldn't stop thinking about a nice ass and a great pair of tits.

But after hours?

We'll see.

See what? If her reserved attitude now was any indication, he had a feeling he wouldn't be seeing a whole lot of Joey. Despite the risks to both of their careers, nothing just wasn't an option he was interested in entertaining.

6

HE'D CALLED HER Joey. In front of nearly everyone in the litigation division, too. She'd noticed more than a few curious glances tossed her way at the use of her family nickname. No one at work ever called her Joey. Only her closest friends called her that. Or her family, but with both of her parents now gone, other than her sisters most of them called her Josephine. It was the Winfield way.

"You don't look like a Josephine," he said.

The way he looked at her, with a way-too-sexy smile and a softening of his gaze as he casually traveled the length of her, was *so not* office appropriate. Neither were her tingling breasts for that matter.

"It's a family name. I was named after my father's aunt." Something her great aunt probably despised since they were nothing alike whatsoever. To Aunt Josephine, appearances were everything, whereas Joey could give a rip what people thought—most of the time. But this was work, and she didn't want people getting the wrong impression of her relationship with Sebastian. Not that they had a relationship, she reminded herself sternly. A mind-blowing, best-sex-she'd-had-in-forever one-night stand did not constitute a relationship. And she'd do well to remember that.

"I would've called you," he said with that sexy grin still in place, "but until this morning, I didn't even know your last name."

She fought hard not to smile at his admission, then berated herself for getting all soft and mushy inside just because he said he'd wanted to call her. Sheesh! What were they? In junior high? Yet she couldn't help wondering, if he'd known she was a Winfield, would he still have called her? Would he be intimidated by her family's wealth? Why did she care?

She desperately needed a distraction before she did something stupid—like get all wound up fantasizing about the really hot phone sex they could've had. "What did you do with Shelby Martin?"

Sebastian frowned. "Who?"

"Shelby Martin. The lawyer whose office you stole."

He chuckled. "I didn't steal anyone's office. Shelby's been relocated."

It was her turn to frown. "Relocated where?"

"She'll be dividing her time between litigation and bad faith."

That was a surprise to Joey. She had no idea Shelby was interested in bad-faith actions. Personally she didn't care much for that area of law. In her opinion, it was the bad-faith division's job to help insurance companies screw over their policy holders by denying claims.

"Why isn't your office up here in the Penthouse? You do realize it's generally unheard of for a partner in this firm to actually work in the trenches."

"I'm more of a hands-on kind of guy," he said.

Was it her imagination or did his gaze actually darken? She couldn't be sure, but her pulse revved just the same.

She cleared her throat. "Shall we get started?" she suggested again.

He nodded and glanced at the list her secretary had provided him. "Tell me about *Renaldo v. Cantoni Motor Sports.*"

"A products liability action," she said, grateful for the distraction. "Herman Renaldo purchased a Jet Ski from our client, Cantoni Motor Sports. He alleges negligence in that our client knew or should have known that the Jet Ski was defective due to a manufacturer's recall. We've filed a cross-complaint against the manufacturer, who in my opinion, is liable."

Sebastian jotted notes on a legal pad. "Has a trial date been set?"

"No," Joey told him. "We're still in the early discovery stages. However, there is a mandatory settlement conference scheduled for late next month. I'm considering filing a motion for summary judgment since I don't believe our client has any liability in this action."

"Have you retained expert witnesses yet?"

"No," she said with a brief shake of her head. "I didn't feel there was a need. While the Jet Ski was defective, the nationwide recall wasn't issued until the day *after* the plaintiff's purchase. Therefore, our client had no knowledge of the recall at the time of the sale so there's no negligence on Cantoni's part."

"Okay, good," he said. "Go forward with the MSJ. Be sure to let Laura know when the hearing is scheduled so she can put it on my calendar."

Joey frowned. "Are you going to take the appearance?" She'd been handling her own motions for the last two years and didn't see any reason why she shouldn't continue doing so. Granted, the stakes were higher in a motion for summary judgment, but she wasn't a total rookie and had previously handled a couple of them on her own. The judge had even ruled in her favor on one of them.

"Probably not," he said and jotted something

down on the legal pad in front of him. "But I will attend the hearing with you."

Her frown deepened. If he was one of those micromanagers, then they were bound to clash. In her first eighteen months with the firm, like any other newly minted lawyer, she'd worked closely with the more senior litigation associates, assisting them with their caseloads. But for the past two years, she'd been assigned her own cases and had grown accustomed to working independently. And dammit, she liked it that way. "Mind telling me why?"

The smile suddenly curving his lips was full of charm, making her instantly suspicious. "You questioning my management style?"

She leaned back in the chair, crossed her arms and gave him a level stare. "Maybe."

"Don't take it personal." He stood and walked to the long row of low cabinets along the wall behind her. "I'll be observing a lot of appearances over the next couple of months, not just yours. I like to get a feel for how the associates handle themselves." He opened a cabinet, then closed it. "Someone told me there was a fridge in here."

"To your left," Joey said. "What you mean is that you want to see if we're in over our heads."

He opened the cabinet door that hid a small refrigerator and retrieved two bottles of water. "Some lawyers think faster on their feet than others," he said, and handed one to her. "I find it helpful to know everyone's strengths and weaknesses when it comes to assigning cases."

Joey thanked him for the water. "Is that why you're taking over the *Gilson* trial? You don't think I'm strong enough to handle it?"

He sat and frowned. *"Gilson?"*

She twisted the top off the water and took a sip. *"Gilson v. Pierce."* Her case. Her most important case, for that matter. One she seriously resented relinquishing.

He scanned the list in front of him. "Trial is scheduled for next week?"

"Yes. Pretrial motions will be heard a week from Friday. Jury selection the following Monday. I should have my pretrial motions finalized by Thursday."

"Sounds as if you're on top of things."

She was, and had the billable hours to prove it. "At the core, *Gilson* is a wrongful death action," she explained, "although the plaintiff is also alleging loss of consortium as a result of her husband's death. Patricia Gilson's husband died while he was having sex with his mistress, Natasha Pierce. I was told on Friday that I was going to second chair you at trial."

"I wouldn't worry about it," Sebastian said,

twisting the cap of his own bottled water. "It'll never see the inside of a courtroom."

He couldn't be serious. Could he? "How can you say that?" she argued. "You don't know anything about the case."

"I know it's a bullshit action that shouldn't have lasted this long."

"I don't think you realize how important *Gilson v. Pierce* is. No matter which way the jury decides, precedents are going to be set."

"Come on, Joey," he said, his tone mildly impatient. "Do you really want to be the lawyer associated with something like that?"

She set the bottle on the conference table a bit more forcefully than she'd intended. "Josephine," she corrected him with narrowed eyes. "And like what? No matter which way this one goes, there will be an appeal. Mass Home and Life has already made it clear if the jury awards so much as a dime, I'm to file an appeal. If we should prevail, and I'm confident we will because it is a bullshit action, plaintiff's counsel has already promised to appeal the decision. This is a case that can make the books, Sebastian. It's important."

"Important for whom? Every scorned wife whose husband couldn't keep his dick in his pants, or every unscrupulous woman out there poaching on someone else's territory?"

His puritanical attitude surprised her clear down to her Bruno Magli pumps. Not that she really knew him, but considering what they'd done, she hadn't expected him to be such a prude.

"Does it matter when we have an opportunity to set a precedent?" she asked.

"Yes, I think it does."

She crossed her arms over her chest. "You're making a moral judgment."

"And you're not?" he challenged.

"No. I'm looking at the legal ramifications of the case. Isn't that what a good lawyer is supposed to do?

"A good lawyer looks out for the best interests of his client. Pierce's insurance carrier is our client. We might represent the mistress, but our *client* is…"

"Mass Home and Life," she supplied. "But I still think you're being dictated to by your morality. You can't do that, Sebastian. Yes, our job is to serve our client, but we also serve the law."

"And we'll best serve the law by never letting this case go to trial," he said, his gaze steady. "We lose and we'll be setting a precedent all right, for anyone who's ever been cheated on to file a lawsuit. You tell me, how is that in our client's best interest?"

She understood what he was saying, even if she didn't agree with him. However, even she had to admit he did have a point. Sort of. A loss in court could possibly cause a negative domino effect. On the loss-of-consortium issue alone, scorned spouses everywhere could end up suing the other woman or man. Insurance carriers would be inundated with new lawsuits. Policy holders would eventually feel the brunt as well, come policy renewal time, with yet another price hike. But what if she won? Would the victory still be as sweet now that Sebastian had muddied the morality waters?

"Mass Home and Life isn't willing to settle," she informed him. "Perhaps you should review the file before issuing any edicts."

He let out a rough sigh and scrubbed his hand down his face. "I'm not trying to be unreasonable."

She reached for her bottle of water again. "Sure you are. You're the new guy. You need to make an impression. Let us all know who's the boss."

"That's not fair, Joey. I'm just doing my job."

"Do me a favor," she said. "Familiarize yourself with the case first before making a final decision. I'd really like to take this one to trial."

"To serve our client? Or yourself?"

"Oooh," she said with a manufactured chuckle. She took a drink of water, then added, "Now who's not being fair?"

It wasn't that *Gilson v. Pierce* was a career-maker as Sebastian was implying, but no matter which way the jury decided, the case could definitely end up being a historical decision. Once it went to appeal and the appellate court ruled, depending upon the outcome, she could even end up arguing before the Supreme Court. Well, probably not her, more than likely one of the senior partners, or even Sebastian, would do the actual arguing. But she'd be the one to prepare the writ, and that appealed to her, as it would any attorney.

He shot her an agitated look, then stood and strode to the bank of windows. Outside, heavy snow had begun to fall from the dark, gunmetal grey sky, swirling in the brisk winds blowing through the city. With his back to her and his hands tucked into the front pockets of his trousers, she admired his ass.

Suddenly, he turned back to face her. He didn't smile. In fact, he didn't look particularly pleased with her at the moment. Not that she cared. Much.

"Get me the files and I'll take a look," he told her. "No promises, Joey."

She let out the breath she hadn't even realized she'd been holding. "Fair enough."

He returned to the table, and she resumed briefing him on her caseload. As a three-year associate, she didn't have a huge number of cases, but by the time they were finished, she understood why the partners had brought Sebastian into the firm. The man had a brilliant legal mind. Unfortunately for her, she'd always been a believer in smart being sexy.

Still, by the time she walked back to her office about an hour later, other than his continuing to call her Joey despite her protestations otherwise, and his initial comment about calling her, he'd kept their meeting professional. Heaven help her, she should be thrilled, but damn if she didn't feel the tiniest dent to her feminine pride just the same.

"MR. SAMUEL'S SECRETARY just came down to let us know he's closing the office early because of the storm. If you don't mind, I'd like to go, too, before it gets too bad."

Sebastian looked up from the file he'd been reviewing to glance out the window. It wasn't quite four o'clock, but sure enough, the storm that had been predicted had arrived in full glory. "No problem," he told Laura. "Did we get the files on *Gilson v. Pierce?*"

"I received them about an hour ago," Laura said as she set two thin pressboard files on his desk. "There are three full boxes on the floor by my desk."

"Thanks, I'll get them. What's this?" he asked, indicating the new files.

"*Waterston v. Markel* and *Johannson v. Play Write Toys.* New cases we just got in that you need to assign to the associates. *Johannson* is a products liability action and *Waterston* is a straight liability against a homeowner. A swimming pool leaked onto the plaintiffs' property and caused damage. Both have answers due next week."

He leaned back in his chair and stretched his legs out under his desk. He'd been reading case files for the better part of the afternoon and was starting to feel it in his back. Nothing an hour at the gym wouldn't cure.

Laura gathered up the stack of documents he had sitting in his outbox. "If this storm is as big as has been predicted," she said, "chances are the office will be closed tomorrow, too."

"If this thing doesn't end soon," he said with another quick glance out the window, "the entire city will be shut down before midnight." Which meant he needed to pack his briefcase before leaving so he could work from home just in case. "Guess that means I'll see you when I see you, then."

"Guess so," she said and smiled. "Do you need anything before I take off?"

He shook his head. "No, I'm good."

She turned to leave, then stopped. "Oh, I almost forgot. Jo wanted me to tell you that she has a meeting scheduled with Natasha Pierce Friday afternoon for trial prep. She thought you might want to sit in."

Jo. He didn't like it. Joey wasn't a Jo or a Josephine. She was, well, Joey.

"Go ahead and put it on my calendar." He had a call in to the insurance company's case manager. With any luck at all, they'd be telling Pierce there would be no trial. "Good night, Laura."

"G'night, Mr. Stanhope."

"Laura?"

She paused at the door. "Yes?"

"It's Sebastian." The partners preferred formality, but his shirt wasn't all that stuffed. Partnership or no, it was the reason he preferred to have his office down in the trenches with the associates rather than upstairs with the other partners. Between that and his open-door policy, he'd already caused a few eyebrows to raise with the other junior partners. He wondered how many of them were already looking for office space in their own divisions.

Once Laura left, he stood and walked to the window. From his vantage point eleven floors up, he could see the streets below were already a mess. The sand trucks had been through, turning the accumulating snow into an ugly brown mush, slick and dangerous, before the plows could remove it. In the distance, he spied the red and blue blinking lights of emergency first responders. Heavy traffic with commuters attempting to get out of the city wasn't helping the situation that was only bound to get worse.

He'd been smart to buy the SUV, and the four-wheel drive would come in handy on a night like this one. Not that he had all that far to drive.

He turned back to his desk and picked up the two new files Laura had dropped off before leaving. His first instinct was to assign the products liability case to Joey, but he held back. Because he feared the appearance of favoritism, he wondered? Perhaps he was simply being *über*-sensitive, but he hated that he was doubting himself where his decisions regarding her were concerned. And he'd only been on the job a matter of hours.

He had twenty-two associate attorneys under his command, all handling a variety of litigation matters. Her caseload was considered light by firm standards, less than twenty-five active files, but she was only a three-year associate. And in addition to her own small caseload, she still supported two other more senior associates who had more cases than they could handle alone. Granted, she was a young attorney, but in his opinion, from what he'd seen thus far, she was capable of the additional workload.

The firm he came from in Miami handed out cases based on who was next in the lineup. He preferred to make his assignments based on an attorney's strengths. Plus, he had two additional associates with even less seniority than Joey, with only a handful of their own cases to consider as well. And then there were the lawyers with more seniority, all of whom were eager for new cases.

He opened the *Waterston* file. Determining the complexity of the case at such an early stage wasn't all that difficult, especially considering the plaintiffs' counsel had named several defendants in addition to the homeowner. Whoever handled *Waterston* would need to have strong organizational skills because the case threatened to become a paper nightmare with a lot of expert witnesses.

He pulled out the spreadsheet Laura had prepared for him in order to get a better feel for the balance of the workload in his division. Shelby Martin was out of the question, since he'd already promised her he'd reassign half of her current litigation caseload to make room for all the new bad-faith actions she'd be covering.

Dillard Bowman could easily handle it. He was a twelve-year senior associate and a bit of a kiss-ass with a minor chip on his shoulder for being passed over for promotion. During the luncheon meeting he'd had with the senior partners today, they'd made no secret that Bowman had wanted

Sebastian's job, but according to Lionel Kane, they hadn't felt Bowman was management material.

Shane Henley or Penny Thurman would do a good job, for that matter, as both had ten years behind them. Thurman had more experience with geological issues, but from what he'd assessed about her personality thus far, she wasn't anywhere near as anal as Bowman.

So that left Henley or Bowman.

Or Joey.

He blew out a frustrated stream of breath. He shouldn't be wasting so much time worrying over a damn case assignment. Or more accurately, worrying over what rumors might crop up if he assigned Joey a new case. He suspected that his calling her Joey in front of the other associates this morning had already caused a few tongues to wag, and from the brief flash of panic in her eyes, she'd known it would happen, too.

He hated office politics. He hated even more that he had to pretend they weren't…what? Involved? They weren't. Not really. They'd slept together. Period. He'd be stupid to start something with Joey. He thought he should probably forget Friday night, but he couldn't. He liked her, a lot. He wanted to spend more time with her, get to know more about her. She was smart, sexy as hell and tried real hard to come across as a bad girl. He already knew how she liked her eggs, that she was a hard rock fan and that the backs of her knees was one of her erogenous zones. But what he didn't know was if she was interested in getting to know him better.

Of course there was only one way to find out—appeal to that bad girl she tried so hard to be. He leaned back in his chair, laced his fingers behind his head and imagined all the erotic possibilities.

7

JOEY PULLED HER coat tighter and shivered, and she hadn't even stepped out of the building. She peered through the floor-to-ceiling windows of the lobby. Tall banks of snow already lined the street, which was filled with cars at a standstill. She'd never make it out to Brookline in this weather.

Oh, poor Molly, she thought. Left to her own devices again. Maybe she could sweet talk Louise, her grandmother's housekeeper, into sneaking over to the carriage house to make sure Molly's food and water dishes were sufficiently filled.

With any luck, she might be able to make it as far as Katie's, where she could bunk for the night, but the roads were such a mess, she had her doubts. She should've left the office hours ago, but no, not her. Was making an impression that important? Fat lot of good it had done her, now that she was stranded in the city for the night.

She set her heavy briefcase down at her feet and

fished her cell phone out of her purse to call Katie. Her sister answered on the second ring.

"I've been waiting for you to call me back all day," Katie scolded without greeting. "What happened?"

"I'll tell you everything later."

"When are you coming home?" Katie asked, a hint of desperation in her voice. "I need rescuing."

"Oh, God, where are you?" Joey asked, immediately concerned for her sister's safety. "You didn't try to drive in this mess, did you?"

"Not quite." Katie lowered her voice to a hushed tone. "I'm trapped in Brookline because of this stupid storm. Help."

Joey let out a big sigh of relief. She'd envisioned Katie stranded in the storm, her car buried under tons of wet, heavy snow. "What are you doing out there? You knew this storm was coming," she scolded.

"Luncheon with Grandmother."

Joey smiled at the defeated tone in her sister's voice. "Oooh, wedding plans already?" Katie and Liam hadn't been engaged a week and already her grandmother was hell-bent on turning Katie's wedding into the society event of the year? Her sister's life was going to be nothing short of hell until she said *I do*.

"It's not funny. But if you must know, Grandmother wanted to discuss the preliminaries for the engagement party."

Joey shuddered. She could just imagine the blue-blooded spectacle *that* would be, probably second only to the actual wedding. "Better you than me."

"Your sympathy takes my breath away," Katie complained. "Keep it up, Joey, and I'll make sure your bridesmaid's dress is *pink*."

"Okay, okay," Joey said with a laugh. Katie knew how much she despised the color pink. "I'll try to be more sympathetic in the future. Look, I'm stuck in the city tonight. If you can tear yourself away from all those bridal magazines for a minute, could you sneak over to the carriage house and make sure Molly has enough food and water?"

"Better yet, I'll go bunk with her," Katie suggested. "I could really use the break. If I stay here, Grandmother will have me picking out china patterns before much longer."

"I hope you know I'm trying really hard not to laugh right now."

"I knew I could count on you for support," Katie said dryly. "I have Duke with me. Molly hates him."

Duke was Katie's adorable cocker spaniel. "She'll get over it," Joey said. "Thanks, Katie."

"Hey, wait. What happened with Mr. Boss Man? Did you survive?"

Joey let out a groan at the memory. "You mean, other than my graceful entrance?" She told Katie about her mortifying experience of literally crashing into the conference room this morning. "All in all, it wasn't so bad. I can see why the senior partners brought him on board." Even if she didn't agree with his assessment of the upcoming *Gilson* trial. His position surprised her, and she couldn't help but be curious.

"Yeah, but what about…you know?"

"Nothing to worry about." She winced at the sudden sharpness of her voice. "We were both completely professional," she said, although she still felt the slight sting of disappointment even if that's exactly what she'd wanted.

Or had she?

She let out another sigh. "I don't suppose you have a key hidden somewhere so I can get into your place for the night, do you?" She really didn't want the hassle of trying to find a hotel room, but it was looking as if she didn't have much choice in the matter. On a night like tonight, she imagined she wasn't the only commuter stranded in the city.

"Sorry. I gave it to Liam, who by the way, is stranded at O'Hare Airport until this damn storm clears," Katie said. "What are you going to do? You're not going to try to drive home are you?"

Joey looked through the windows again. A dark blue sedan skidded to a stop—and slid right into the snow bank. "Not a chance."

Behind her, an elevator dinged. She glanced over her shoulder just as Sebastian stepped into the lobby. He saw her and grinned, then headed in her direction.

"Don't worry about me," she told her sister. A slow smile tugged at her lips. "Something tells me I'm gonna be just fine."

"ON NIGHTS LIKE THIS, I have to say even though I feel guilty for thinking it, I sometimes regret not taking one of the offers I received from those firms out in Los Angeles. They have much better weather."

Sebastian dragged a French fry through the glob of ketchup on his plate. "Don't feel guilty." God knew he was feeling guilty enough for both of them at the moment. Inviting Joey to his place to wait out the storm probably wasn't his brightest move, but when he'd found her in the lobby as he was leaving the office, it wasn't the head above his shoulders he'd been thinking with. One smile from her, coupled with a sassy comeback filled with innuendo, and he'd lost all common sense.

He popped the fry into his mouth, then wiped his hands on the paper towel and tossed it on the plate.

"I checked the weather forecast for Miami before I left the office. It was in the eighties there today."

"Homesick already?" Joey asked with a laugh.

"Only for the sunshine."

She laughed again and something deep inside him stirred. His heart? Impossible. Or was it? He'd never felt anything like it before and couldn't be certain. Still, he wondered at the cause.

Maybe it was the sparkle in her blue eyes when she looked at him, or the delicate turn of her hand when she slipped a loose strand of hair behind her ear before she bit enthusiastically into her cheeseburger from the take-out place on the corner. Whatever the cause, he knew he'd be better off ignoring it. Only he couldn't, even if both of their positions at the firm might depend on it.

"I bet you had a lot of firms trying to recruit you," he said.

She slid off the wooden stool at the breakfast bar and carried both of their plates to the sink. "Oh, and you didn't?"

He gathered up the remnants from their impromptu take-out dinner and carried them to the cardboard box still doubling as a trash can. "I'm not the one who graduated from Harvard Law. Top five percent of your class?"

To say he'd been impressed by her background

had been an understatement. Although in reality, he hadn't been all that surprised. Friday night he'd pegged her as having money. He just hadn't realized her net worth would make his look like a pittance in comparison.

"Not top five percent, but top *five*." She rinsed their plates, but when she looked at him over her shoulder, a frown creased her brow. "Who told you?"

He leaned his hip against the counter and gave her a sidelong glance. "Think about it."

Her eyes instantly widened. "You snooped in my personnel file?"

"I snooped in the personnel file of everyone who works in my department," he said, then winked at her. "But I read yours more carefully."

She snapped her mouth closed, then after a moment's hesitation, shook her head and smiled at him. "You really *don't* play fair, do you?"

He grinned. "I believe in taking advantage of the resources available to me." He pushed off the counter. "More wine?"

Her smile turned positively wicked. "Are you trying to take advantage of me?"

"Would you mind?"

"Not in the least," she said. "Besides, what else are we going to do during a snowstorm?"

That's what he liked best about Joey—her

honesty. She was refreshing in that she didn't appear to be the type to play head games or turn everything into a drama. She was the last woman on earth he should consider becoming involved with in a relationship, but he was beginning to think she just might be worth the risk.

He refilled their wineglasses, still nothing more elegant than cheap red plastic tumblers, but she didn't seem to mind. Something else he admired about her. Although he'd learned she was a Winfield, one of "the" Boston Winfields, with roots dating back all the way to the *Mayflower,* she was unpretentious and down-to-earth.

She dried her hands on a paper towel, then smiled her thanks as she took the refilled tumbler from him. "I see you've made some progress since I was here last."

"Some." He inclined his head to the dining area off the kitchen, where several packing cartons took up the small space. "We could finish unpacking my kitchen," he suggested. "Then maybe I could offer you wine in a real glass for a change."

"It's what's in the glass, not the glass that counts." She took hold of his hand and led him from the kitchen to the living room. "Is that thing for real or just for show?" she asked, indicating the gas fireplace.

Lighting the fireplace was as simple as turning

a knob and adjusting the level of the fire. "Good thing it's gas," he said as he slid the screen closed, "or we'd have to resort to burning the furniture."

She sat in the middle of the sofa, toed off her shoes and curled her feet up beneath her. "What it lacks in authenticity, at least it makes up for in atmosphere."

He joined her on her sofa. "You want atmosphere?" He reached over and flicked off the lamp, setting the room in darkness lit only by the flames flickering in the fireplace. "How's that?"

"Hmmm. Nice," she said and snuggled up beside him.

Cozy, he thought. And comfortable. Too comfortable for the last two people who should be sharing wine in plastic cups in front of a fire during a snowstorm together.

He let out a long, slow breath and settled his arm around her shoulders. "What are we doing, Joey?"

"Sitting in front of a fire and enjoying a glass of wine after feasting on a take-out dinner of greasy cheeseburgers from the only place in your neighborhood that was still open."

"That's not what I meant."

"I know," she said quietly. "But can't we just enjoy the moment? Do you really want to ruin a nice evening with reality?"

"Our reality is that we not only work for the same firm, but I'm your immediate supervisor," he reminded her.

"Not the sexual harassment thing again. You know, it's only harassment if one of us complains." She tipped her head back to look up at him. The light in her blue eyes warmed his heart. "If you haven't noticed, I'm not complaining."

Yet. But what would happen when he did something to piss her off? Joey was a passionate person. They were bound to clash eventually. Would they be capable of keeping the bedroom out of the office? Or vice versa?

Only time would tell, he supposed.

"And if you're really worried, for the record, I practically invited myself tonight."

He didn't know about that. When he'd stepped off the elevator and noticed her standing in the lobby, the last thing he'd thought of were the ethics involved in their seeing each other outside of the office. "Are you suggesting I merely offered you safe harbor from the storm? Now who's taking advantage of whom?"

"Is that what they call it down south?"

"What do you Yankees call it?" Little did she know, he, too, was a Yank. A minor detail he figured would come up eventually if they continued down the path he was certain they were traveling.

That wicked smile of hers returned, firing his blood. "Sex."

His body instantly responded. "Yeah, that's what we call it, too," he said, then dipped his head and lightly kissed her lips.

She angled her head to deepen the kiss, but he pulled back. There'd be plenty of time to make love to her later. She wasn't going anywhere tonight—Mother Nature had made sure of that.

She looked at him with an odd expression on her face, then shifted her position and leaned back against him and faced the fire. "Since you already seem to know so much about me—because you cheated by reading my personnel file—tell me something about you."

"I lived in Florida."

She gently nudged him with her elbow. "You didn't grow up there," she said. "That's no Floridian accent you got going there, Stanhope. It's subtle, but it's still New England."

"I grew up not far from here," he admitted. "South Boston."

"A Southie? I never would've guessed. I was thinking maybe Cambridge," she said. "My half sister owns a bar in South Boston. So do you have brothers? Sisters?"

He shook his head, then realized she couldn't see him. "An only child."

"Uh-oh, not very good at sharing your toys, are you?" she teased.

"Hardly," he said, unable to completely keep the edge of bitterness from his voice. His mom had done her best, but there hadn't been a whole lot of money left over each month for many extras. "Half sister?"

"Three sisters total," she told him. "Lindsay is my half sister, but I grew up with Brooke, who was the oldest until a few months ago when we learned about Lindsay, and finally Katie, the youngest."

"Did Lindsay live with her father?"

"No." She pulled in a deep breath and let it out slowly. "My mother gave her up for adoption. Katie's the one who discovered Lindsay. We didn't know about her until after my mother passed away last summer."

He tightened his hold on her. "I'm sorry," he said.

"Thank you," she said quietly. "I miss her."

She took a sip of wine and stared at the fire, momentarily lost in her own thoughts. He held her close, enjoying the feel of her body against his.

"You said Lindsay owns a bar on the south side," he prompted after a few moments.

"Yes," she said. "Chassy. Nice place, actually."

"Do you have a relationship with her?"

"We're trying." She let out a sigh. "She's a little standoffish yet, but I think it's because she's just trying to keep from getting hurt. We come from very different backgrounds, and I don't know that it's really an issue with Lindsay, but to be fair, we Winfields can be a little overwhelming. Especially when we travel in a pack."

In all honesty, he couldn't blame this half sister of hers. The thought of being bombarded by three Joey-types would scare the hell out of anyone. "Be patient," he advised. "It couldn't have been easy for her."

She took another sip of wine. "She's the one who had it easy in my opinion, but I doubt she'd see it that way. She didn't have to deal with all the crap we did."

"Do you think she resents you and your sisters?"

"God, I hope not. We might not have wanted for anything, but being a Winfield isn't always easy. Everything Lindsay has, she's worked for, and I admire her for that. A lot. We all do. At least Brooke, Katie and I do. My grandparents haven't even spoken Lindsay's name yet."

"Maybe she just needs more time."

"That's what we're hoping." She leaned forward and set her empty cup on the table, then shifted on the cushion beside him and turned to face him. "So, tell me, Sebastian. South Boston. Stanhope. Doesn't quite match up. I guess that means you're no relation to Emerson Stanhope."

"He's my father."

Curiosity lit her gaze. Had bitterness crept into his voice again? He wouldn't be surprised considering he despised the son of a bitch.

She tilted her head slightly to the side. "But…?"

"But we're not close."

"So I gathered."

He let out a sigh, wondering how much, if anything, to tell Joey. He wasn't a bastard, but he might as well have been. "He and my mother were married for a brief period. I don't think I was quite a year old when he left her for another woman, one considered more suitable, and took his Stanhope dollars with him."

A frown creased her brow. "I'm sorry," she said, her tone sympathetic.

"Don't be," he said and downed the last of his wine. "I'm not."

"Yes, I can see that."

He shrugged. "I have the pedigree, but not the trust fund."

Her frown deepened. "Unless you're a show dog, pedigrees don't mean squat. At least to me they don't. Or to my sisters."

The chill that surrounded his heart whenever he talked about his father, which wasn't often, thawed at the conviction in her voice. "What is important to you, Joey?"

She reached out and stroked her hand down his chest. "Pleasure," she said in a husky voice filled with warmth. "Especially the kind we can give to each other."

He liked the sound of that. But… "For how long?"

Her hand stilled. Something flashed in her eyes. Fear? Funny, but he had difficulty imagining Joey afraid of much of anything. Caution, perhaps? That he understood.

"What exactly do you mean?" she asked carefully.

He wasn't certain what he meant, but what the hell? He was the one who'd turned down this road, he might as well see it through to the end, wherever or whenever that might be. "I think you know what I mean."

She laughed suddenly, but the sound was slightly brittle. Forced, even. "Until we're both too exhausted to move," she said and slipped her arms around his neck. "Or the storm lets up. Whichever occurs first."

Before he could issue an argument, she urged him forward and brought their mouths together in a hot, openmouthed kiss. A kiss, he'd bet, that was meant as a distraction. For now, he thought as he gathered her close and deepened the kiss. Later she'd have to face the same truth that he'd suspected their first night together—that a casual relationship was out of the question. And sooner or later, they'd have to deal with the fallout.

8

JOEY KNEW SOMETHING strange was happening to her, something she'd never felt before. Not altogether certain she welcomed or feared this odd sensation occurring deep within her, she didn't yet know. What she did know, however, was whatever was happening between her and Sebastian extended the bounds of basic physical attraction. Who knew exactly where it might lead them, or if she even wanted it to go beyond a physical relationship? But for now, the latter was all she was willing to accept.

Atop the cushions from the sofa, which Sebastian had spread on the floor in front of the fireplace, Joey straddled him. Drawing warmth from his big body that the throw he'd placed over them barely provided, she reveled in the feel of him. Skin to skin. Woman to man. His hardness to her softness. She wasn't about to get in to the whole yin and yang thing, but damn, she didn't think heaven on earth could get much better than this.

"I take it back," she whispered against his ear. She smoothed her hands over the width of his chest. "I love snowstorms."

"Beats the hell out of a heat wave," he said, then kissed her deeply.

His hands held her bottom where he gently kneaded, his long, strong fingers pressing rhythmically into her flesh. She ended the kiss and placed a trail of light kisses of her own along his jawline, his throat and down to his chest, where she whorled the tip of her tongue around his nipples. His soft moan of pleasure encouraged her to continue her sensual exploration.

Slowly, she tasted her way down his torso. She used her hands and her tongue, sliding her hands down his sides to his waist, over his belly and lower. Sifting her fingers through the springy curls surrounding his length, then taking him in her hand. He felt hot and heavy. She flicked her tongue over the tip of his penis and his hips jerked in response.

He didn't dare try to stop her, but he did guide her gently around so she was straddling him again. When she took him into her mouth, the warm hiss of breath he expelled brushed against her moist heat, sending a spiral of desire curling through her.

He dipped his fingers inside her, gently thrusting and retreating, spreading the moisture from her body over her already-slick-with-need flesh. She worked him with her lips and tongue, loving the taste of him, the way his breath quickened with each stroke of her mouth over him.

He teased her with his tongue and nearly sent her crashing over the edge. She took him more deeply into her mouth, returning the pleasure. He suckled her clit and, far too quickly, the tension growing inside her snapped and she came.

He gave her no time to cool, but gently lifted her and positioned her on her back. She opened her legs and hooked her ankles around his waist, drawing him down. With a lift of her hips, she welcomed his long, hard length inside her. A slow, gentle wave of fresh desire cascaded over her.

In the firelight flickering over their bodies, she looked into his dark-eyed gaze. The tenderness in his eyes stilled her breath as did an affection she instinctively knew exceeded their mutual physical attraction. An attraction, she suspected, that extended beyond caring to one she feared the most—the bloom of a deeper and possibly even lasting emotion. The kind that practically guaranteed she'd end up with her heart in tatters when they parted ways.

She clung to him. He murmured soft words she refused to process, so she closed her eyes and concentrated on the erotic motion of their bodies, lost herself in the giving and taking of pleasure. It was all she wanted, she told herself. All she could emotionally afford. She didn't want forever. She'd played that game once and lost, and she had no desire to experience that kind of heartbreak again. She only wanted the danger and excitement of the forbidden. She only wanted *this,* for as long as it lasted.

The intensity of their lovemaking climbed with each stroke of his body into hers. The muscles in his back and arms strained from the climbing tension. She moved her hands to his ass and held him to her as she arched against him. Together they came in an explosion of heat and, dammit, a myriad of emotions she refused to acknowledge were anything but sexual in nature.

COLD AND IN DESPERATE need of caffeine, Joey drummed her fingertips on the ceramic-tile counter, impatient for the coffeemaker to finish brewing. Wearing a battered Florida State T-shirt and a pair of thick wool socks she'd commandeered from Sebastian's dresser, she shivered against the chill of the early morning.

She opened a few cabinet doors before she finally found a couple of coffee mugs. A check of the refrigerator produced a rare treat of flavored creamer. She loved the stuff, but usually avoided the extra calories.

The coffeemaker finished and she splashed some of the chocolate-raspberry creamer into the mug, then filled it nearly to the brim with hot, steaming coffee. She brought the mug to her lips and breathed in the rich, aromatic scent before taking a tentative sip. She moaned with pleasure. One thing she could say about Sebastian, the man had excellent taste.

In the mood to splurge, she searched the cabinets and unearthed a box of strawberry Pop-Tarts, but no toaster. Hungry, she snagged a package anyway.

With mug and breakfast pastries in hand, she left the kitchen and strolled over to the long windows of the living room. Snow blanketed the North End, giving the revitalized neighborhood a shiny, pristine glow that even the dark, gunmetal-gray skies couldn't dim. Snow still fell lightly, but it looked as if the winds had died down a knot or two.

Another shiver passed through her. Damn, but it was chilly. She set her bounty on the coffee table, then turned on the gas fireplace and cranked it up to high. Instant warmth radiated from the hearth, and she took advantage of the heat, standing with her back to the flames.

Once the chill finally left her, she stooped to pick up the cushions and return them to the sofa. After making love, they'd lain in front of the fire and had fallen asleep holding each other. Sometime later, during the early morning hours, Sebastian had gently woken her and they'd gone to bed, where they'd made love again while the fierce winter storm had continued to rage outside.

Gathering the throw around her, she settled on the sofa with her coffee and turned on the television in hopes of catching the local weather forecast. A ticker scrolled across the screen announcing closings for the schools and several government offices in the area, while the morning anchors talked of a series of incidents throughout the night caused by the storm. The news turned to sports and talk of the upcoming Patriots' play-off hopes against the Pittsburgh Steelers.

She sipped her coffee and waited for the weather report. She wasn't sure exactly when she'd be able to make it out to Brookline, but she did have an idea or two on how she and Sebastian could pass the time until the roads were cleared.

Being embroiled in a good old-fashioned office romance did have a few perks, especially when Mother Nature provided the perfect foil for playing hooky. Still, she did worry that someone was bound to get hurt eventually, and the law of averages dictated it'd more than likely be her.

Could she still work with Sebastian when this thing they had came to an end? She hoped so because she loved her job and would hate to leave the firm. She'd specifically accepted Lionel Kane's generous offer for employment because of the firm's reputation and long history, and she'd hate to give it all up because she couldn't keep her panties on whenever she was around Sebastian. And because Sebastian was now a partner in the firm, she seriously doubted he'd be the one to go elsewhere anytime soon.

She ripped into the package of Pop-Tarts and snacked. What if, by some bizarre twist of fate, she let down her guard long enough for their relationship to become serious? In her opinion, their relationship was still in the booty-call stage…sort of, except she had a bad feeling Sebastian might actually feel otherwise. Then what was she supposed to do?

She was a litigator. So was he, for that matter. He'd been hired to head up their litigation department and she was a junior partner in one of the city's oldest law firms. Were they destined for disaster?

Probably so, she mused, taking another sip of coffee. At least professionally. She had no interest in transferring to another division. Corporate law bored her. Family law depressed her. The only thing worse than probate and estate planning was real estate law, which would be a fate worse than death in her opinion. Word would eventually get out about their affair, no matter how hard they might try to keep their private life private. The rumors would spread like wildfire, she was sure. What would the senior partners have to say about it? Probably, neither of them would be fired or even censured, since the firm didn't have a fraternization policy, but she imagined the partners would not be happy.

So then what? Personally speaking, that is. What if they made the stupid mistake of actually falling in love? She let out an exasperated puff of breath. Not that she imagined something like *that* happening. But still, she couldn't help *but* think about it.

As she polished off the second Pop-Tart, the news finally switched to the weather forecast and she looked on with interest. The meteorologist predicted the worst of the storm had passed, but another four to six inches were still expected to fall in the area throughout the day. She had work to do, but suspecting she wouldn't be in today because of the weather, she'd packed several files in her briefcase before leaving the office last night. With a no-travel advisory in effect, it looked as if she was stuck at Sebastian's for the time being.

Oh, for shame, she thought with a smile.

Maybe she should go hunt up her briefcase now instead of wasting time worrying about a bunch of what-ifs that might never arise. Besides, she had a bigger problem she'd like to resolve. Like how to get around Sebastian's moral judgment so she could take *Gilson v. Pierce* to trial.

On the surface, Natasha Pierce could easily be construed as an unsympathetic defendant. She hoped that once he had a better understanding of the case and the issues involved, he'd see that the defendant really wasn't the evil hussy that he was painting her to be.

She was no more of a fan of infidelity than Sebastian, although after last night's conversation, she certainly had a better understanding of his opinion on the matter. An opinion he was more than entitled to, but one she could not allow to color his judgment of the case.

Although Sebastian hadn't specifically stated it, it sounded as if his father had made no attempt to see his son or even offer financial support. That itself was odd, unless his mother had refused financial support. Another oddity, as raising a child alone couldn't have been easy, but she imagined his mother's decision more than likely stemmed from pride than anything else.

That Sebastian resented his father was obvious, and that saddened her. She couldn't imagine what it would be like being cut off from her family, especially her sisters. Okay, so maybe she wouldn't exactly mourn for too long if her nasty cousin Eve, whom they called Evil-Lyn behind her back, fell off the face of the earth. Especially after she took such delight in outing Brooke's unfortunate striptease faux pas, but that was her deep sense of sisterly loyalty talking.

With a frown, she uncurled herself from the sofa and went in search of her purse and cell phone. Armed with a fresh cup of coffee, she hurried back to the warmth of the throw. Despite the early hour, she called Brooke.

"What do you know about this dare I'm supposed to get on Thursday?" she asked as soon as Brooke answered.

Her sister laughed. "Is that really why you called me at seven in the morning?"

Busted. Brooke knew her too well. She needed someone to talk to and she always turned to one of her sisters.

"Yes and no," she admitted. "But I do want to know if you've heard anything about my dare. Katie is having just a little too much fun at my expense." She took a sip of coffee. "And just so you know, I won't be taking my clothes off in public, either, if that's what you guys are thinking."

Brooke groaned. "Will I ever live that down?"

Joey giggled. "Probably not. Expect a recounting of events, with the proper embellishments, at holiday dinners for say, oh…the next thirty years or more. Just think how you can embarrass your children with the threat of a striptease."

"Grandmother will be so thrilled," Brooke said, her voice infused with humor.

Joey laughed again.

"I don't know about your dare," Brooke told her. "According to Lindsay, each dare is a highly guarded secret until the official unveiling."

"But you tried."

"Not even two Mistletoe Martinis could get it out of her," Brooke said. "So where are you? I talked to Katie last night. She said you were stranded in the city."

"Well—" Joey cleared her throat "—I wouldn't be calling the Four Seasons to leave a message for me anytime soon."

Brooke gasped. "You're at his place? Oh, Joey, what are you thinking?"

"Oh, don't you dare sound so scandalized, Brooke Winfield, when I know darn good and well you're with David right now."

"Not at the moment."

Brooke sounded way too cagey to appease Joey. "What? He down at the corner buying bagels?"

Brooke sighed. "Something like that. But I'm not the one with a job at stake here."

"My job is not at stake," Joey argued. "I mean, having an affair with my boss probably won't get me a promotion anytime soon, but it's not like we're violating firm policy."

"What about ethics?"

"Nope." There was nothing unethical about her affair with Sebastian. "People have flings with co-workers all the time."

"Then what's the problem?"

"Who says there's a problem?"

"You called me at seven in the morning."

Joey let out a weighty sigh. "I like him."

"And this is a problem because…?"

"Brooke? Have you not been paying attention? He's my boss."

Okay, so she realized she was making little sense. But wasn't that what sisters were for? To make sense for you when your ability to do so yourself was seriously skewed? Like now?

"I mean, seriously," Joey continued. She plucked at a loose thread on the throw. "Where can this possibly go?"

"Anywhere you're willing to let it go," Brooke said sagely. "Hey, isn't there some statistic that says something like forty-two percent of married couples met on the job? Maybe it's forty-eight percent. I don't know. Check it out on Google. You'll see."

Joey let out a sound of disgust. "You've been so helpful. Goodbye, Brookie."

"No, wait. Is that what you're afraid of?"

Joey frowned. "I'm not afraid of anything," she said, without a modicum of conviction.

Brooke mumbled something Joey didn't catch, but she imagined it wasn't flattering.

"Just because Carson Baker was a slime doesn't mean Sebastian is."

Joey winced at the sound of Carson's name. How could she have believed she'd been in love with him? "We're having an office romance, Brooke. No one is talking serious relationship here." She let out another sigh. "It'll run its course and that'll be it. We're both mature adults. We'll handle it. Right?"

"You know what they say," Brooke said with a distinct hint of laughter in her voice. "'Tis better to have loved and lost—"

"God," Joey groaned. "Spare me. Please."

"Just trying to be helpful."

The sound of running water drifted into the living room. "Sebastian's up. I'll call you later," she said, then added, "when we come up for air."

"Joey? Would it really be so bad if this turned into something more?"

Joey thought about that for a second before answering. "I don't know," she admitted. "That's what scares me."

"I thought you weren't afraid of anything."

"Anything but love," she said, then flipped her phone closed.

9

"Is that coffee I smell?"

"It is."

Sebastian headed into the kitchen for a cup. When he'd awoken alone, he'd initially thought Joey had been more successful in pulling another disappearing act, sneaking out without waking him. Until he'd heard her voice, talking on the phone, he assumed, to one of her sisters.

God help him, he'd actually relaxed knowing she'd stuck around. The fact that she'd stayed during the light of day actually gave him hope that she thought of their relationship in terms other than physical.

Joey intrigued him, no two ways about it. She could be as skittish as a colt one minute, then open and honest and almost brash the next. Not that he minded the many sides to her multifaceted personality, but he'd like to know more about her. Such as why she retreated behind sarcasm, for one.

As he came back into the living room, she set her

cell phone on the end table. "Looks like we're snowed in for the day," she said. "There's a no-travel advisory in effect, so I'm betting the firm is closed."

He had no problem with that, if it meant being snowed in with Joey. Although he would've liked to have spent the day in the office. There were associates he had yet to meet with, more new cases to assign— which the receptionist had delivered to him before he'd left for the day—and plenty of open case files in the late discovery stages he wanted to review. He had brought a few files home with him, but he'd have preferred to work at the office, only because he had yet to set up his home office. As it was, his laptop was sitting on the dining room table and he had no Internet connection, which meant he wouldn't be able to do any research of the *West Law* database from home.

He dropped down on the opposite end of the sofa from Joey and kicked his feet up on the cushion next to her. She took one end of the throw she'd bundled herself in and covered his feet.

"There," she said, and gave his feet a gentle little pat.

When he gave her a questioning look, she shrugged. "I'm cold," she said before taking a drink from her own mug.

He glanced at the fire blazing in the hearth then back at Joey. "So that means I'm cold, too?"

She cradled her mug in her hands and nodded. "It's a rule."

He smiled. "A girl rule."

One of her eyebrows winged upward. "You got a problem with girl rules, Stanhope?"

He rested his arm on the back cushion. "Only in that you never know if you're breaking one until it's too late. A guy can get into a whole lot of trouble that way."

Her expression was lofty and clearly indicated she was a pure, blue-blooded Bostonian through and through. He suspected it wouldn't be much of a stretch to assume she'd learned it from the cradle, her being a Winfield and all.

"If your kind would get with the program," she said, her tone starchy yet teasing, "then it wouldn't be a problem, now would it?"

"You should publish a volume of these rules. Annual updates would be helpful, too. Like *Massachusetts Rules of Civil Procedure* or the *Federal Reporter.* Less confusing for us mere mortals that way."

She made a sound of mock disgust. "That would never work. How would we keep you off balance?"

"Now that's the beauty of it," he reasoned. "We'd be on the same page."

She slipped a hank of honey-blond hair behind

her ear. "Where's the fun in that?" she teased, then flipped the channel to the *Today Show*.

He settled back and drank his coffee with the realization that he adored this side of Joey. Sweet and teasing, sassy and sexy as hell, wearing…he peered closer…one of his old T-shirts. And only his T-shirt, he mused, since a pair of black lace panties were currently drying on the towel rack in his bathroom.

His body stirred, making the jeans he'd slipped into feel a little too confining. He shifted his position on the sofa slightly. Once the commercial break came, he asked, "So, what are we supposed to do with ourselves all day?"

She let out a sigh and turned to face him. "Gee, I have no idea." Her tone remained light and carefree, although her expression said she had plenty of ideas on exactly how they could pass the time. "Maybe go build a snowman?"

He had a few ideas of his own and it didn't include snowmen. In fact, he wouldn't mind suggesting a few to her, as well. "Whatever we decide on," he said, "we have one small problem."

"Shortage of condoms?"

He chuckled. "No. Food."

"Yes, I noticed. Old Mother Hubbard would feel right at home." She turned her attention back to the television set.

He nudged her thigh with his toe. "I'm hungry," he complained.

She ignored him in favor of Matt Lauer.

He nudged her again. "I'm serious."

She swatted at his foot. "You're on your own, pal," she said with little sympathy. "I already had myself a feast this morning. Chocolate-raspberry creamer and strawberry Pop-Tarts. Yum."

"There's a market on the corner, but who knows if they'll be open."

"I realize you've been gone a while, but need I remind you, this *is* Boston. It takes more than a few gazillion feet of snow to keep us down for long. Besides, I know for a fact there's a bagel place open. When I talked to Brooke, David had gone out for bagels."

"Is that your sister's husband?"

"No. Well, not yet anyway, but it is serious," she said before taking another sip of coffee. "Katie, Lindsay and I have a pool going, though, on how much longer it'll be before Brooke ends up married to Boston's most notorious bad boy. If they elope before the season starts, I win."

Confused, he frowned. "You lost me." Unless she was referring to the social season, then he really could care less. But there'd been a time when he had cared, and had even resented that he'd been excluded from his rightful place in Boston society.

She let out a sigh. "David Carerra is my sister's boyfriend."

"Carerra? The baseball player?"

"That would be him."

"I'd heard he was invited to spring training camp."

"Thank heavens," she said. "We sure as hell don't need another season like the last one."

Ah, so she was a sports fan. He liked that. Not that he was a fanatic, or anything, but that meant she wouldn't get herself into a snit if he wanted to watch the occasional game.

"What about your other sisters?" he asked. Not that he was really all that interested, but he was curious about her and liked learning more about her.

"Katie's newly engaged to Liam James. Poor thing spent the day with our grandmother yesterday going over preliminary plans for an engagement party. I'll bet my secret chocolate stash has been emptied."

"You live at home?"

She shook her head. "Heavens, no." She offered up a shudder of mock revulsion. "My place is on my grandparents' property, though. Katie stayed there last night since she was caught in Brookline by the storm, hence the suspected raid of my emergency chocolate supply."

"If you have your own residence, it can't be all that bad."

"It's not really. Brooke is the one that has it rough. She lives in the house we grew up in, which is right next door to my great aunt."

"And what about your other sister?"

"Lindsay?" At his nod, she said, "She's married to Chassy."

"Let me guess. A football player."

She laughed. "No. Chassy is the bar she owns."

He remembered, now that she'd mentioned it. Somewhere over in South Boston, he thought.

"What about you?" he asked, foregoing subtlety for hard-core information. "Ever been married?"

"Nope. Close once, though."

"How close?"

"Day-before-the-wedding close."

That didn't sound good. "What happened?"

"My fiancé had a major character flaw, so I called off the wedding."

"Let me guess. He didn't like cats."

"Almost as bad," she said with a slight edge to her voice. "He hadn't stopped dating."

He knew the type. Emerson Stanhope had been a cheating bastard. "I'm sorry. That had to be rough."

She shrugged, but he could tell from the flash of irritation in her eyes that her pride still felt the sting of betrayal. "It was at the time…when I caught him in bed with two of my bridesmaids." She manufactured a saccharine-sweet smile. "You?"

"Nope," he said with a shake of his head. "No bridesmaids."

She gave him a frown and nudged him with her foot.

"No," he said with a chuckle. "I've never been married."

"Engaged?"

"Never."

"Close?"

"Not really."

"Well, if you're gay, then you've sure managed to fool me."

He chuckled. "I've been told I work too hard." And that had been one of the nicer things his last girlfriend had said about his workaholic tendencies.

"Need a life, do you?"

"So I've been told."

She leaned forward and set her empty mug on the coffee table. "Are you really starving?"

"I'm withering away here. Can't you tell?"

She swept him over with her gaze. His body instantly responded to her slow, steady perusal. "You look fine to me," she said. "I think I'm hungry after all."

"Un-huh, lady," he said jokingly. "No nookie until you feed me. I need sustenance and you ate already."

She shrugged off the throw and stood. "A non-toasted breakfast pastry does not constitute a meal. What do you say we go find us an open greasy spoon in the neighborhood, then come back here and figure out an interesting way to pass the time?"

He stood as well. "I brought work home with me. I should at least make an attempt to get through some of it today."

"Gee, me, too," she said, then flashed him a high-wattage smile full of sass. "I'd hate to have my new boss thinking I'm off screwing around all day."

He grabbed hold of her hand and gave a gentle tug, pulling her to him. Her arms went around his waist and she lifted her lips to his for a quick, hard kiss.

"That, my dear," he said, "depends on who you're screwing around with. And since it is your boss, I'd say you don't have too much to worry about."

"WE SHOULD TALK," Joey blurted.

Sebastian looked up from one of the files he'd been working on for the better part of the past two hours. A legal pad, filled with notes and instructions, was positioned precariously on his lap. He'd suggested they could work in the dining room, but she liked being by the fire.

Warmth filled his brown eyes when he looked at her. "It's a known fact that conversations that begin with 'we should talk' are guaranteed to cause indigestion."

"Seeing as we ate over three hours ago, I don't think it'll be a problem." They had found a diner open two blocks over, as well as the corner market Sebastian had mentioned, where they'd stocked up on enough food supplies to last the entire winter. She might be madly in love with her little red roadster, but having a boyfriend with a big SUV came with a few perks.

She closed the file in her lap and set it on the sofa cushion beside her. She'd been working on a status letter to the insurance adjuster in charge of the case, but her concentration kept slipping. "I'm serious, Sebastian."

He picked up the remote control for the stereo set to a Top 40 station, and turned down the volume. "What's on your mind?" he asked as he leaned back against the cushions.

She pulled in a quick breath. "I like spending time with you."

"But…?"

"But it's a problem."

"Because…?"

"Because of our professional relationship," she said, wondering why he was pretending to be so dense. "If word gets out, we might not lose our jobs, but it wouldn't look good. You're a partner. I'm an associate. Hello?"

He let out a sigh. "I know."

She drew in another deep breath. She'd never been accused of being shy, and she didn't think now was a good time to start. "If we're going to continue spending time together, then we should probably set a few ground rules."

He crossed his arms over his chest. "Such as?" he asked with a note of caution in his voice.

"All extracurricular activity takes place off campus."

The grin that slowly spread across his face was nothing short of wicked. The man was impossible.

"Meaning I can't pull you into an empty conference room and have my way with you?"

She rolled her eyes. "Something like that."

"Damn. I was planning on trying that one out tomorrow. Before lunch."

Her shoulders drooped. "Would you be serious? Please?" How did they expect to carry on an office romance on the sly if he wasn't willing to look at the situation with at least a modicum of sincerity?

With his cavalier attitude, they'd be busted by the end of the week.

The wickedness of his grin intensified. "I'm perfectly serious."

She gave him a level stare. "Sebastian."

"All right," he said, sobering. "I get it, Joey."

"That's another thing. You can't keep calling me Joey at the office. You should see the odd looks I get whenever you do."

"You're not a Josephine. Not to me."

She wasn't to her, either, but that was another neurosis best saved for another discussion. "Jo, then."

He shook his head. "Not even close."

"Then call me Winfield," she said a little too snappishly. "Anything but Joey."

"Why? It's your name."

"Because when you call me Joey, it leaves an impression of familiarity that isn't appropriate in the office. People will talk. Before long, they're going to figure it out."

"Figure what out?"

"You're doing it again."

"Doing what?"

"Being deliberately obtuse."

He let out a sigh and reached for her hand. With a light tug, he hauled her into his lap. The file she'd been working on slid to the floor.

"You know what I think?" he asked.

She looked at him through narrowed eyes. "Who knows what goes on inside that man-brain of yours."

He ignored her sarcasm. "I think you're making too much out of nothing. No one cares what I call you. And no one is going to find out we're having an affair."

Affair? That was what they were having, weren't they? Sometime between last night and this afternoon, they'd gone from a sort of booty-call relationship right into an affair. Although they barely knew each other, they were involved. She had to face that fact at least.

Was what they were sharing deeper than mere physical attraction? She'd hazard a guess and say, more than likely. But did she want it to be more? No matter how long she mulled it over, the answers just weren't all that easy for her.

"Unless we start going at it like rabbits on a desk, that is," he added.

She frowned. "But…"

His hands traveled down her spine to settle on her bottom. "Relax, Joey."

She blew out a stream of breath, then looped her arms around his neck. "Okay," she said and attempted to relax her shoulders. "I'll try."

"That's a good girl."

She chose to ignore the mild hint of condescension in his tone. Because if he really knew the real Joey, he'd probably be horrified. Growing up, Katie might have been the one to get into more trouble, but that was only because Katie hadn't learned how not to get caught.

Besides, would a good girl really be having a hot and heavy affair with her boss, of all people? She didn't think so. But that was her, all right. Joey Winfield, bad to the bone, all wrapped up in a pedigree dating back to the *Mayflower.*

"I think I could use some help in that department," she said and wiggled her bottom against him. She felt the hard ridge of his erection through his jeans and smiled. "I am feeling a little tense at the moment."

"We can't have that." His hand slipped behind her head and he guided her to him to nibble on her neck. "How's this?" he asked, the sound a sexy rumble against her sensitive skin.

"Mmm," she murmured. "A nice start."

He used his other hand to sneak beneath the hem of her blouse. His fingers teased her nipples through the lace of her bra, the sensation sending sparks of delight skittering through her limbs. Need tugged at her, and she had every intention of answering the call.

"And this?" he whispered against her skin.

"I have an even better idea," she said, then took his hand and guided his fingers beneath her skirt to where her panties were already damp with need.

"You're so wet," he said, his voice filled with awe. "So hot."

She closed her eyes and arched against his questing fingers, encouraging him to stroke her deeply. Before long, his expert touch had her writhing against his hand as she drew closer to that blissful moment when her world tilted and she came. She cried out, caught by surprise by the unexpected power of her orgasm.

Relaxed didn't begin to explain how she felt. More like boneless. But he didn't give her a chance to recover. He eased her off him and had her on her knees on the sofa, her skirt pushed up around her waist. After quickly dispensing with her panties and freeing himself from his jeans, he entered her from behind in one swift stroke. She felt all of him moving inside her and moaned at the exquisite sensations shooting through her like a series of flashing bolts of lightning on a summer night.

He leaned over her. With one arm banded around her waist, he continued to thrust into her, each stroke of his body more powerful than the last until they eventually collapsed, sated, atop the sofa in a tangle of limbs and disheveled clothing.

She didn't know how long it took for her world

to be righted again. Probably when she couldn't breathe because Sebastian was crushing her. "Air," she said, her voice strained. "I need air."

"Sorry," he mumbled, then sat up and pulled her with him.

She tugged her skirt over her hips and frowned at the wetness between her legs that wasn't completely her own. Turning to Sebastian, she gave him a harsh glare. "Well, that was stupid," she said, unable to believe what they'd just done.

When he didn't look as if he was anywhere close to catching on, she said, "Unless I'm mistaken, and believe me, a girl knows the difference, we did that without protection."

The color instantly drained from his face. "Ah, shit. Joey. I'm sorry."

She stood and scooped up her panties. "We very well could be," she muttered.

God, why had she let that happen? She knew the answer to that one—because she'd been as carried away as he'd been. He wasn't the only guilty party here.

"Look, I know it was stupid, but I'm clean." He stood and fastened his jeans. "I promise you that."

Her blouse hung open, so she tugged it closed. "I wasn't talking about disease, but for the record, so am I."

He scrubbed his hand down his face. They might have dodged that particular bullet, but she still had a big bomb to drop. The kind that could possibly have a fallout neither of them were ready for.

He stooped to pick up the file that had fallen. He straightened and looked at her sharply. "You are on birth control, aren't you?"

Here goes, she thought. Slowly, she shook her head. "Nope. And just to keep it interesting—I'm ovulating."

Ka-boom!

10

BY NOON THURSDAY, Joey still couldn't believe that two intelligent, educated people could have been so incredibly stupid. For crying out loud, she and Sebastian weren't a couple of hormonal teenagers, she thought as she made the turn from Chestnut Hill onto Hatherly Road. Obviously, she was doomed to repeat history, since reckless, impulsive behavior was practically a family trait—at least on the Breckenridge side.

"Talk about the apple not falling far from the tree," Joey muttered, referring to her mother after having gotten pregnant not once, but twice, by the same guy. At least she had better taste in men than her mother, as Sebastian was nothing at all like Nathan Sprecht, the man who'd fathered both Lindsay and Brooke. Although her own father, John Winfield, had been quite the catch. Maybe her mother hadn't initially married for love—although according to Reba her father had been head over heels for Daisy—but she had grown to love John Winfield. Growing up, it'd been obvious to her that her parents were very much in love.

If it turned out she was indeed pregnant, Joey felt confident Sebastian would be very much a part of his child's life. Not that she had any intention of marrying the man in a shotgun wedding—in grand Winfield style, of course—but she'd never deny him his child. That much she did know for certain. Since they were both reasonable, competent adults, much of the time, anyway, they'd figure a way to make raising a child together work.

By the time she pulled up in front of Reba's house in the quiet suburban neighborhood of Brighton, she was frowning again. A child would greatly complicate her life, but she'd find a way to deal with it. Although she certainly had more choices than her mother had in her day, adoption just wasn't an option she would consider.

It must've broken her mother's heart, making Joey wonder how on earth Daisy had survived knowing she had another daughter she couldn't know. At least she now understood those rare occasions when her mother's mood would turn oddly melancholy. It hadn't happened all that often, but every now and again, she'd catch her mom staring wistfully out into space, her mind elsewhere. She'd ask her mom what she was thinking about, curious about what could make her mother look so incredibly sad, but her mom would just smile at her and say it was nothing.

Joey knew better now. It hadn't been nothing. Her mother had been thinking about Lindsay. Daisy Breckenridge Winfield was such a loving parent, the heartbreak alone caused by giving away a child had to have been devastating, and Joey knew deep in her heart, she could never do it. She simply didn't possess that much courage.

She cut the engine and snagged the bag containing the lunch she'd picked up from the Green Briar Bistro, an Irish pub located right in Brighton not far from Reba's, along with the shopping bag with the Worthington logo that Brooke had dropped off over the weekend. Katie had called her this morning and said that Reba was feeling a little down in the dumps, so Joey hoped the lunch from the pub would perk her mother's best friend up a bit. Besides, she'd wanted to get out of the office for a while and what better way to spend an hour or so than talking with her mom's colorful friend, Reba.

The front door swung open before Joey reached the steps leading up to the front porch. "Move your scrawny behind, Chicken, before my own tuckus freezes and falls off."

Joey smiled at the nickname Reba had called her for as long as she could remember, one she'd earned because Reba had said when Joey was born, her legs were scrawnier than a chicken's.

She didn't know why Reba was complaining. The weather had improved greatly since Monday's storm, although the temps were still hovering in the mid-to-low twenties. At least the snow had finally stopped falling and the roads were more than passable.

As she climbed the steps to the porch, Joey took in Reba's outrageous outfit. Reba still had a relatively slim figure for a woman her age, and she took pride in showing it off. Today she wore a pair of figure-hugging black stretch pants tucked into a pair of decade-old, stylish, fur-topped boots. A wide black patent-leather belt cinched her waist, and a black-and-hot-pink geometrically designed top showed off her medically enhanced bust line. A shrug, made from some sort of fuzzy fabric that made Joey sneeze when she leaned in to place a kiss on Reba's overly made-up cheek, completed the outfit.

"It's not so bad today," she said, then lifted the bag with the bistro's logo on the front. "I brought lunch."

Reba took the bag containing their lunch and ushered her inside the modest home she shared with her husband, Darwin. The place was a tad too small and cluttered with mementos collected over nearly six decades for Joey's tastes, but she did enjoy the comfortable, kick-off-your-shoes-and-relax atmosphere of Reba's home.

"Where's Darwin?" Joey asked, not seeing the missing link residing on the sofa as Brooke had claimed he'd been doing since retiring last fall. "I hope you didn't chase him off, because I brought plenty of food for the three of us."

"He's supposed to be at the gym," Reba said with a stern expression. "Doctor said if he didn't start exercising, he was gonna die. I said if he didn't do something, I was gonna kill him."

"It's good he listens to his doctor. Most men don't bother."

"Yeah, well, don't hold your breath. He's no doubt snuck off to O'Leary's, choking on a boatload of BS with the other Boston Bocas. I told him if he didn't start doing something besides watching the Western Channel all day, I was going to trade him in for a pair of thirty-year-olds."

Joey tried to hide a smile and failed. "I guess he took you seriously."

"He'd better," Reba said. "He's become such a fixture on that damn sofa, I took the feather duster to his balding head the other day."

Joey laughed. "Retirement requires an adjustment

period." She dropped her purse on the chair beside a coat tree in the foyer, then hung her coat and scarf.

"Oh, Chicken, you don't know how much. It's been a stretch of my patience." Reba looked pointedly at the bag with the Worthington logo. "Whatcha got there?"

"More of Mom's things Brooke thought you might like to have," she said and placed the bag on the chair.

Reba handed Joey back the bag containing their lunch and peered inside the one with the things Brooke had sent. She plucked the top item from the bag and carefully unwrapped the tissue, revealing an understated, soft blue cashmere twin set. A wistful expression transformed Reba's face, momentarily eliminating the harshness of too much makeup used in an attempt to cover up nearly six decades of a hard life. To say that Reba came from modest means was an understatement.

"I was thinking about your mama just this morning." A note of sadness entered Reba's voice, rough from too many years of smoking.

Joey figured as much, based on the phone call she'd received from Katie a few hours ago. "I know," she said. "I've been thinking about Mom a lot this week myself." More than she was willing to admit to Reba, or anyone, at this point.

Reba returned the sweater set to the shopping

bag and tossed a quizzical glance at Joey. "Everything okay, Chicken?"

Joey nodded. "I'm fine. Just missing her."

Reba let out a long sigh. "Losing your mama leaves a big ol' hole in all of our hearts, baby girl. It's gonna take time."

Before they could slip into a maudlin conversation, Joey quickly manufactured a bright smile. Her quest here today was to cheer Reba up, not have them both diving for the tissues. "We should enjoy some of this food before it gets cold." She aimed for bright, but landed a little too close to brittle instead. "I'm starved. What about you?"

She turned and wound her way through the overcrowded living room to the kitchen, knowing Reba would take the hint and follow her. The kitchen, a bright yellow menagerie of tag-sale tacky meets country charm, wasn't nearly as crowded as the living room. She set the bag on the round table of indistinguishable wood with a Nevamar top near the window and started removing the take-out containers.

"That sure smells good." Reba appeared at her side with plates, cutlery and a roll of paper towels to serve as napkins. "Whatcha got there?"

"Enough to feed an army," Joey said cheerfully. "You won't have to cook tonight if you don't feel like it." She started opening containers and setting them out on the table. "I brought clam chowder."

"Of course, you did," Reba said dryly, then went back to the cabinet, returning with two mismatched bowls for the soup. "Did you get those appetizers I like so much? The boxty wedges and Irish sausages? With the cheddar cheese dip?"

Boxty wedges were nothing more than potato cakes, deep-fried and served with a warm cheddar sauce. They were Reba's favorite so Joey had made sure she'd ordered extra.

"Sure did. I figured Darwin would be joining us, so I picked up their full appetizer platter, too." Joey put the empty bag near the garbage can by the back door. "And a couple of their triple-decker pub clubs. I thought you and I could share one, since they're so huge."

Joey pulled out a chair and sat. Through the open curtains, she looked on at the barren, snow-covered backyard, which was typically Darwin's domain. For a retired bowling ball salesman, he possessed uncanny gardening skills. During the spring and summer months, he magically transformed the small space into a virtual haven from the sheer urban-ness of the city.

She looked at Reba, who was enthusiastically enjoying a miniature Irish sausage. "Maybe Darwin should consider a part-time job in a flower shop. Or maybe at a green house. Something part-time wouldn't affect his Social Security benefits."

Reba popped another sausage into her mouth. "That would require motivation on his part."

Joey smiled at that. "You could update your threat."

"To what? Three twenty-year-olds?" Reba laughed and licked a dollop of cheddar cheese dip from her finger. "Baby girl, at my age, I just don't have enough time left to do all the training it would take to get them where I like them."

"And how's that?"

Reba gave her cloud of cotton candy yellow hair a pat. "Out of my hair."

"It just sounds as if he's bored," Joey offered. "And what about you? What are you doing to keep busy?"

She listened while Reba related her latest adventures, a belly-dancing class for seniors she'd begun taking two weeks ago at the local community center. Most women Reba's age took up knitting or flower arranging, but then Reba was hardly like most women her age, and definitely not the grandmother type. More like the crazy aunt no one talked about at the dinner table.

"Best exercise I've had in months," Reba said, then patted her flat stomach with pride.

While they continued eating lunch, Reba demanded an update on the Winfield sisters, and then Joey mentioned a couple of the cases she was handling that she thought Reba might find interesting.

"Your mama was so proud of you," Reba told her. "I thought she was gonna bust somethin' when you got into Harvard."

Joey couldn't help but smile at the memory. The day she'd been accepted at Harvard Law School, her mother had been so happy, she'd cried. Both of her parents had been thrilled for her. When Evil-Lyn had attempted to put a damper on their celebration at a family dinner by making a snide comment about Joey's choice of law school and the Winfield's long Yale tradition, her mother had practically spit nails.

Finished with lunch, Joey stood and started clearing dishes, then helped cover the leftovers and carried the containers to the refrigerator. Her hand stilled when she noticed a small beige envelope, about the size of a formal invitation, held by a magnetic clip and tacked to the refrigerator door. She read the delicate script on the envelope, addressed to Daisy Breckenridge.

Curious, she set the containers on the counter and pulled the envelope from the holder. "What's this?" she asked Reba.

The dishes in Reba's hands clattered in the sink. "Shit," Reba muttered. She rinsed her hands, then dried them on a dish towel. "Let's forget you saw that, okay?"

"Let's not." Joey reread the return address and frowned. "Why would Elegance Escort Service be sending something to my mother at your address?"

Reba made an attempt to snag the envelope, but Joey, being a good four inches taller, easily held it out of reach. Reba's laugh was little more than a nervous twitter. "It's not important."

"Obviously it is." Why else would Reba suddenly be so jumpy? "Are you going to tell me or do I open it?"

"Damn," Reba swore. "I could sure use a cigarette right now." She opened a nearby drawer, withdrew a blister pack of nicotine gum and popped two pieces into her mouth.

With the envelope still in her hand, Joey quickly stashed the leftovers in the fridge then turned back to Reba. "Talk to me."

Reba let out a breath so long and slow, the fuzzy threads of her hot pink shrug ruffled as if swept by a summer breeze. "You'd better sit down, Chicken."

Dread filled Joey. From the way Reba was now wringing her hands, whatever she had to say couldn't be good.

Hadn't they had enough surprises since their mother's death? First their discovery of the daughter their mother had given up for adoption, followed by the truth that Brooke and Lindsay shared the same father, a fact Brooke was still wrestling with to some degree. Who knew so many skeletons could be packed in one woman's closet?

Joey carried the envelope with her to the table and sat. Once Reba did the same, Joey gave her a pointed look. "I'm waiting."

"I told you, it's not important," Reba said in a rush. "It's just an invitation. I got one, too."

"An invitation to what?"

"A reunion…of sorts."

Joey's patience was slipping fast. "What sort of reunion?"

"Look, Chicken, your mother left that life behind when she married your father. No little girl grows up dreaming of that kind of life, but it happens. And your mother didn't have a very good start. Hell, none of us did. It was a different time when we were growing up. There weren't a bunch of busybody social service people running around trying to save every displaced child. We did what we had to do to survive."

Joey dropped the invitation on the table as if it burned. "What are you talking about?" she asked, her exasperation evident in the sharp note in her voice.

Reba chewed frantically on her nicotine gum.

She crossed her arms over her chest. "I'd appreciate an explanation, Reba."

The other woman chewed some more, then turned to look out the window. "Your mother never wanted you girls to know."

Joey's patience bottomed out. "Know what?" she demanded more hotly than she'd intended.

Reba appeared even more nervous, if that were possible.

"Reba," Joey said, softening her tone. "Please. Just tell me. Whatever it is, it can't be that bad." She hoped, but feared otherwise just the same.

Reba turned back to face her with a pained expression in her eyes. Suddenly, she looked every one of her sixty years. "Your mother and I worked for Elegance Escort Service."

Joey's world tilted, then spun. She gripped the edge of the table for support. She couldn't have spoken if her life depended on it. She suspected it just might, too, as she stared at Reba, dumbstruck.

"For a couple of girls from the wrong side of the tracks in Providence," Reba said, her voice surprisingly steady, "it seemed like a good idea at the time."

"But…*why?*" Joey asked eventually. She kept her iron grip on the edge of the table out of fear she'd topple out of her chair.

"What can I say?" Reba shrugged. "We were

young and honest to God, we didn't know any better. We were offered a roof over our heads, knew where our next meal was coming from and the money wasn't half-bad. It sure beat the hell out of standing on a street corner in the middle of winter."

"Oh my God," Joey whispered. "You were *call girls?*"

"No!" Reba reached out and grabbed hold of Joey's forearm. She gave her a squeeze Joey suspected was supposed to be reassuring, but her body had gone numb. She barely felt Reba's touch.

"Heavens, no," Reba said with a shaky laugh. "We never took money for sex. *Never.* Elegance was a high-class, legitimate operation."

Joey looked at Reba dubiously. Having known Reba all of her life, she held serious doubts about the class part of it. Reba was tacky and brash, and she loved her to death. Her mother had, too. She'd been Daisy's best friend, but she secretly suspected her father had merely tolerated Reba's presence in his wife's life.

"I swear it, Chicken. *Never.* Your mama vowed she'd not end up like your grandmother, trading her sorry body for spare change. And she didn't, neither. Sure, we had some girls who did the deed for cash, but it was on the sly. Betsy Staple would've fired them in a Boston second if she'd heard about it, too.

That kind of thing was never a part of the services Elegance offered. But your mama, she kept good on her word and did real good for herself, too. Why, she landed your daddy, didn't she?"

Joey stared at the invitation, afraid to touch it now. What other secrets could it possibly hold?

She understood Reba's misplaced words were merely an attempt to soften the blow she'd just dealt. Yet, Joey couldn't get past the fact that her mother was a professional escort.

Good God, how was she supposed to tell her sisters something like this? Brooke was having enough trouble coming to terms with her parentage and still hadn't reconciled with their grandparents. And what about Lindsay? Although Linz had never said a word, Joey suspected her newly discovered sister felt the difference in their economic backgrounds. But to find out their mother was a professional escort? It was too much.

Suddenly Joey looked up from the invitation. "What did you just say?"

Reba looked confused. "What part?"

"My grandmother." She felt physically ill. "What did you say about my grandmother?"

Reba looked stricken. "Forget I said anything."

Joey shook her head. "It's too late," she said. "Reba? Was Daisy's mother a prostitute?"

Reba tipped her head back and looked at the ceiling. There were no answers there. Joey knew.

A dozen heartbeats later, Reba looked her in the eye and said, "Yes, Chicken. She was."

11

By Thursday afternoon, Sebastian had made a decision in the *Gilson* matter. Nothing he'd seen in the file had him leaning toward taking the case to trial, but he did have a better understanding of their client's refusal to settle. Patricia Gilson had no case.

What she did have, however, was a good lawyer, one with a reputation for winning difficult cases. Gilson was suing for $2.5 million in damages and thus far, had refused to consider a settlement offer for a penny less. Even if she prevailed, all she'd receive would be an award the equivalent of the defendant's policy limits. And with it being a bullshit case, one worth no more than nuisance value—a nominal sum usually paid out to make a case go away—Mass Home and Life's refusal to offer the policy limits made sense.

He scribbled a few more notes on the legal pad at his elbow. Joey would not be happy with his decision, but it wasn't his job to make her happy—

at least not when it came to the business of practicing law. Off campus, as she'd called it, was another matter entirely.

They hadn't been able to spend any time together since Tuesday. Last night he'd stayed late in the office until his dinner appointment with the three senior partners. The meeting had gone well, and the partners had been suitably impressed when he'd informed them he had plans for bringing in new business to the firm. In addition, he'd advised them that the firm had been added to the list of counsel representing Mass General, which meant he'd be responsible for medical malpractice actions where the hospital was being sued for negligence.

All in all, it'd been a productive meeting. But when he'd gotten home close to midnight, he was struck by how quiet and empty his apartment had felt without Joey's presence.

Pumped up from the meeting, he'd rattled uselessly around the apartment for a while. He'd thought about calling her, but seeing as it was after midnight, he opted to unpack the last of the moving cartons that had been stacked in the dining room instead. By the time he'd wound down enough to go to bed, he'd ended up tossing and turning for half the night.

As ridiculous as it seemed, after just two nights, he realized he'd grown used to having Joey beside him when he slept. He missed her burrowing under the covers, her slender curves pressed against him. No one had been there to steal his pillow, or tuck her feet near his for warmth. He'd even felt mildly lost when there'd been no one to beat him to the shower in the morning. Not that it mattered since he'd join her anyway.

Man, he was losing his grip. He didn't need the distractions of a relationship, not now when he was supposed to be making an impression to reassure the partners they'd made the right choice in bringing him on board. But damn if he wasn't counting the hours until he and Joey could be together again.

Which wouldn't be until tomorrow night, he realized with a stab of disappointment. She had plans for tonight, but she refused to discuss exactly what, other than to say it was a girls' night out with her sisters.

Never in a million years would he have dreamed he'd be embroiled in a hot and heavy affair with someone like Joey. She was everything he wasn't, and everything he'd resented growing up. She represented what he and his mother had been denied because they hadn't been deemed good enough by the almighty Stanhopes. Joey was old money Beacon Hill, he was working-class Southie. She was Harvard Law, he was Florida State with a good six years left to pay on his student loans.

Their socioeconomic differences didn't seem to faze her, but he couldn't stop thinking about them. Even more so now that there was a possibility she could be pregnant. There wasn't a snowball's chance that he'd allow any child of his to go through one iota of what he had.

Not that his kid would want for anything if he could help it, but he'd be damned if he'd allow the Winfields to make his child feel as if he or she wasn't good enough. Although he had yet to meet them, from some of the things Joey had said about her family, with the exception of her sisters, the Winfields were just a little too reminiscent of the Stanhopes in his opinion.

The thought of having a baby with Joey didn't frighten him. He knew he'd make a good father, and her a good mother. But he had been stunned when she'd admitted she wasn't on any form of birth control. When she'd told him she hadn't had a serious relationship in over a year, and didn't see any reason to put her body through the hell of synthetic hormones, he'd understood. And damn if some part of him wasn't thrilled that she hadn't been seriously involved with anyone else for a while.

He picked up the phone and dialed Joey's extension, but was bumped directly to her voice mail, so he went in search of her. Her office was empty, and her secretary, Mary, wasn't at her desk, either. Tapping the legal pad impatiently against his leg, he walked the short distance back to Laura's desk, positioned outside his own office.

She looked up from the document she was typing and smiled. "I should have these interrogatories done soon," she said.

"I'm not worried," he said, and he wasn't. In the few days he'd worked with Laura, he'd learned she was more than competent, and twice as knowledgeable as half the paralegals the firm employed when it came to civil procedure.

"Any idea where Joey might be?" he asked Laura. Good thing Joey wasn't around. She'd give him one of those I-told-you-not-to-do-that looks for calling her Joey in the office. He didn't get it, but it was her quirk and she was entitled to it.

"Let me check." She switched screens to the master calendar with a few mouse clicks. "She has no appearances this afternoon. She's probably at lunch. Do you want me to let her know to see you when she gets in?"

"No," he said, then changed his mind. "Yeah. Tell her it's about *Gilson v. Pierce.*"

Laura nodded, then pulled a message book from one of the trays stacked on the corner of her desk.

"Anything else?"

"Could you try to get the adjuster on the phone for me?" he asked, then turned and walked back inside his office.

No matter which way he looked at the case, he just didn't see a reason to go to trial. If all the plaintiff would be awarded were the policy limits, what was the point? Trial was expensive, and with the billable hourly rate Samuel, Cyrus and Kane charged, two or three weeks of trial could end up costing the insurance carrier twice as much. Insurance companies thought in terms of dollars and cents, not groundbreaking, precedent-setting case law. If he appealed to their bottom line, he was confident they'd authorize him to make a settlement offer to the plaintiff, and hopefully, the case would go away. Of course, getting the plaintiff to accept a reasonable offer was another matter entirely.

Laura buzzed him to let him know the adjuster wasn't in the office, but she'd left a message for him to return Sebastian's call. He thanked her, then ended up taking a few more telephone calls on his own cases. He dictated a status letter to the client on another matter and was in the process of dictating a list of discovery documents he wanted prepared on yet another case when Laura buzzed him again, advising him Joey had finally returned to the office close to ninety minutes later.

He finished his instructions on the file he'd been working on, then went to talk with Joey. He found her bent over her secretary's desk, scribbling something on a notepad. Inappropriate or not, he swept the length of her with his gaze. She wore a navy pin-stripe suit that flattered her figure to perfection. The skirt wasn't too short, but offered just enough length to give him more than a glimpse of her spectacular legs, which were made even more appetizing by the flame-red pumps she wore. Her suit jacket hung open, giving him a glimpse of a silky top in the same bold shade as her shoes.

Her hand visibly trembled as she slipped her hair behind her ear, revealing a simple gold hoop earring. She must have sensed him near, because she looked up suddenly, obviously startled.

His heart lurched in his chest at the pained expression on her face. She didn't say anything, but shook her head then walked, a bit unsteadily he noticed, into her office and closed the door.

"Hold my calls," he instructed Laura, then headed for Joey's office. He walked in without knocking and quietly closed the door behind him.

He found her seated behind her desk, looking pale and…lost. Concern rippled through him. "What's

wrong?" It couldn't be about their possibly pregnancy issue. As far as he knew, it was too soon, seeing
as they'd had unprotected sex only two days ago.

"Not now, Sebastian." She spun her chair around
to face the window. "I can't talk to you right now."

Her voice sounded thick, as if she were on the
verge of tears. Something had upset her and he was
determined to find out what.

"Is it one of your sisters?" Considering how close
she and her sisters were, it was a natural assump-
tion. Plus, he doubted work would evoke such an
emotional reaction from her.

She laughed, but the sound was hollow, not filled
with her usual exuberance. "In a manner of
speaking, but not like you're thinking. As far as I
know, they're all fine."

Since she wouldn't turn back to face him, he
moved around the desk to crouch down in front of
her. "What happened, Joey? Talk to me, sweetheart."

She looked at him with anguish-filled eyes. "I
can't."

The tremor in her voice squeezed his heart.
"You're sure no one is hurt?"

"Not yet," she said wryly, then shook her head
again. "No. It's nothing like that." She drew in a
deep breath and let it out slowly. "I just need a little
time, okay?"

He settled his hands on her knees. "Whatever it is, you can tell me. I'm right here. I'm not going anywhere."

The hint of a wistful smile touched her still pale lips. "Thank you." She lightly traced her fingers over his hand that still rested on her knee. "I'll be fine. I promise." She drew in another deep, shuddering breath. "Eventually," she added. "I just need some time to wrap my head around something."

He really wanted to push her, wanted her to open up to him and get whatever was troubling her off her chest. He wanted to see her smile, a real one that made her blue eyes sparkle. The kind that had the power to reach deep inside him and brighten his world.

But this wasn't about him, so he backed off, sensing she really did need time to assimilate whatever it was that had her so shaken. He considered pulling her into his arms to hold her close, letting her know she wasn't alone with whatever she was facing, but they were at the office and he knew she wouldn't appreciate such inappropriate behavior here. He might not like the restrictions, but he would respect her wishes.

"Whenever you're ready." He gave her knee a gentle squeeze and stood. "Why don't you come by my place tonight?"

"I can't," she said and spun her chair back

around. "I have this thing with my sisters tonight. I promised."

"Afterward," he suggested, hoping he didn't sound too desperate.

She slid a file closer and flipped it open. "It could be late."

He offered up a careless shrug. "I'll wait up."

That smile barely teased her lips again, giving him a shred of hope. "I'll call you when I'm ready to leave."

"Good enough." It wasn't. Not really, but he had no choice but to settle for less because that was all she was willing to give him.

"WHAT'S THIS?"

"An Amorétini," Denver, the assistant manager at Chassy said of the martini he'd set in front of her. "It's the January M and B drink special."

"Thanks." Joey took a tentative sip. "Oh," she said. "It's a French Silk Martini." One of her favorites, too, a combination of vodka, Chambord raspberry liqueur with a splash of pineapple juice.

As much as it pained her to do so, she reluctantly set the drink back on the bar. "How about a ginger ale tonight, Denver? On the rocks."

"You don't like it?"

"Oh, no. It's perfect." She offered him a smile

she was nowhere near feeling. She really could use a drink, too. Probably two or three, four for that matter. But she didn't want to—just in case. In two weeks though, provided she got her period, she had every intention of getting ripped. Until then, she was doing the right thing and playing it safe.

"I've got to be in court first thing in the morning," she lied easily.

"Suit yourself," he said with a shrug. He took the drink away and returned with a glass filled with ginger ale on ice.

Joey smiled her thanks then took a sip. The bubbles of the ginger ale tickled her nose. She considered pulling out her cell phone and calling Sebastian, but she didn't know what to say to him any more than she did her sisters. Would he care about her mother's notorious past, she wondered? Would it make a difference to him that their possible baby was the descendant of a lady of the evening and a professional escort who didn't have the sense not to fall victim to a smooth-talking cad, not once but twice?

Somehow, she didn't think so, she thought with a small smile. But was she willing to take the risk of finding out? Sebastian was a Stanhope, but in name only, she reminded herself. There wasn't a pretentious bone in the man's magnificent body.

Today when he'd come into her office, he'd been

so concerned about her, she'd almost told him the truth. Her heart stuttered at the memory of how tender, how caring he'd been. It was in that very moment that she'd felt herself falling hard for him, too. Was it love? She honestly couldn't state with any degree of certainty. She figured time would eventually tell the truth on the matter.

She frowned. The truth. Boy, did it ever have a way of eventually revealing itself.

Tired of her own company, Joey took another sip of her drink and set the soda back on the black granite bar. Since she couldn't drink away her sorrows, maybe she could drop a few quarters in the jukebox, fire up a few sad country songs and cry in her ginger ale. But she didn't think the effect would be quite the same without massive quantities of alcohol.

She spun around on the leather-and-chrome bar stool and looked around Chassy. She'd left the office a little later than expected tonight and, as she'd suspected, the happy hour crowd was in full swing, the Beaumont Street bar buzzing and filling up fast.

Lindsay had turned the once run-down, little neighborhood bar into quite the elegant little night spot. Japanese lanterns added a quiet ambiance that was belied by the raucous laughter coming from a table of women near the jukebox. Joey recognized the women as club members from the meeting she'd attended when Brooke officially joined Martinis and Bikinis.

She looked away, but not before Tanya, a plump, giggly and perky redhead, caught her eye and waved her over with her usual exuberance. Joey hesitated for a split second, considering pretending she hadn't seen Tanya. But when one of the other women—Sherry, she thought her name was—stood and bellowed her name followed by a demand for her to move her skinny ass, she didn't have much choice in the matter without appearing rude.

"Don't worry, they won't bite," came a soft, yet steely voice behind her. "Too hard, anyway."

Joey gave Tanya the "just a sec" sign and turned to find her half sister standing behind her. Once again, Joey was taken aback by how much Lindsay looked like Brooke. Or vice versa she supposed, since Lindsay was officially the firstborn.

"You sure about that?" Joey took a sip of her ginger ale. "Sherry could cause a lot of damage with those nails if they grow much longer."

"I wasn't sure you were going to make it," Lindsay said. "Katie thought you might back out at the last minute."

She would've liked nothing more. "Me? Back down from a challenge? Never." Joey tried to appear offended, but from the curious expression in Lindsay's eyes—that were so much like Brooke's it was scary—she knew she was doing a lousy job of pulling it off. She'd taken quite a blow today and was having a hell of a time recovering.

How did one recover from the news her lineage included a ten-dollar hooker and a professional escort? No wonder she was doomed. At least she came by her own bad-girl tendencies honestly.

Lindsay looked pointedly at the glass of soda in Joey's hand. "You're not drinking?"

Joey offered up a wan smile. "I had a little something at lunch that didn't agree with me." Boy, was that ever an understatement.

Lindsay grinned suddenly. "Not nervous about tonight are you?"

Joey attempted a laugh. "Not in a million, sister."

A brief shadow fell across Lindsay's eyes, making Joey immediately regret her word choice. She understood. They were sisters, but they weren't. They might share a biological bond, but no matter how welcome the three of them tried to make Lindsay feel, there would always be something separating them. History.

Some history, she thought as Lindsay made an excuse and went behind the bar. The one they did share, Joey wasn't sure she should even reveal. What good could possibly come from letting Lindsay, Brooke and Katie know about her mother's colorful past? What would she even tell them? Mama came by her disreputable career choice naturally? Or how about, did you know our granny was a whore? Yeah, that would be an icebreaker, all right.

With no other distractions, she left her place at the bar and crossed the room to where Sherry, Tanya and another woman, a tall, slim brunette whose name Joey couldn't immediately recall, sat waiting.

Sherry pulled out a vacant chair. "Take a load off."

"Thank you," Joey said and sat down. "I'm sorry, but you are…"

"Lauren," the brunette supplied. "Tanya tells us you're officially becoming a member tonight. Congratulations."

"Don't congratulate me yet," Joey said. "I have to fulfill my obligation first."

Tanya giggled. "I can't wait to see what Lindsay has in store for you."

Joey produced a mock shudder that felt all too real. "Neither can I," she said dryly.

She glanced toward the doorway just as Brooke and Katie came into the bar. Reinforcements, she thought with equal measures of relief and apprehension. She pasted a smile on her face and hoped her sisters wouldn't notice anything was amiss.

She waved Brooke and Katie over to join them. Tanya caught sight of Katie's engagement ring, and thankfully the attention was all on Katie.

Brooke brought two chairs over from a vacant table and positioned them on each side of Joey. Brooke sat, then leaned close. "What's wrong?"

"Nothing," Joey lied and nearly choked on the guilt. "Long day is all."

"You look tense." Brooke picked up the glass in front of Joey and took a tentative sip. "You're drinking soda?"

Joey shrugged. "A bad lunch," she said, more truthfully. She took her soda away from Brooke and frowned. "Get your own."

After all the oohs and aahs from the women at the table over the size of the rock Liam had put on Katie's finger, her youngest sister plopped down in the other vacant chair. "You look like hell, Joey. What's wrong?"

"Gee, thanks. You always wow Liam with that kind of charm? No wonder he proposed," she said sarcastically.

"Don't be pissy," Katie said, then snagged Joey's glass. She took a drink and wrinkled her nose. "God, that's awful. Lindsay hire a new bartender or something?"

"It's ginger ale," Brooke said.

Concern filled Katie's expression. "You aren't nervous about tonight, are you?"

Joey let out an impatient sigh. "I'm not nervous. I'm not sick. And I'm not being pissy," she complained. "I have an early appearance tomorrow, that okay with you?"

Katie frowned at her. "You are, too, pissy."

One of Brooke's eyebrows winged skyward. "I thought you said lunch didn't agree with you."

Joey let out a frustrated puff of breath and stood, prepared to leave. Brooke grabbed her arm and tugged her back down to her seat.

"What is wrong with you tonight?"

Joey looked at Brooke and for the first time in her life, didn't know what to say to her sister. Coming here tonight was a mistake. She should have canceled, but she hadn't wanted her sisters to think she was afraid of some silly dare. And Katie had been so looking forward to her joining the club, she hadn't wanted to let her down.

Sherry snagged Katie's attention again. Brooke leaned closer to Joey. "What is it?" Brooke prompted.

When Joey said nothing, Brooke added, "You're scaring me."

Joey shook her head. "Nothing." She glanced around the table of women who were swapping dare stories with Katie. If she didn't tell Brooke something, her sister would keep hounding her out of concern. She leaned closer to Brooke and spoke in a low tone so the others wouldn't overhear her. "Sebastian and I had unprotected sex the other day."

Brooke straightened. "That could be dangerous."

"Yeah," Joey said. "Since I'm right in the middle of my cycle."

"That explains the ginger ale," Brooke said, concern evident in her voice.

"I thought it wise. Until I know differently."

"Good idea." Brooke plucked a few cashews from the bowl on the table. "Try not to worry," she said, popping a nut into her mouth. "At least until you actually have something to worry about."

Joey managed a small smile for Brooke's benefit. "One good thing. At least I don't have to worry about a dare that includes naked skydiving."

"For now," Brooke said with a laugh, then flagged down a waitress to place a drink order.

Joey sat back and sipped her soda. She probably shouldn't be worried about the dare. The way she figured it, naked skydiving would be the least of her problems.

12

"FIRST WE RECITE the rules."

With all the ceremony of a town crier, Lindsay stood before the rather large crowd, close to two dozen women, and pretended to unroll an ancient parchment. She held up the invisible rules in front of her and recited from memory.

"The members selected to accept their initiation dare have been approved by a majority of the membership present here tonight. Joey Winfield and Angela Barker," Lindsay said, giving each woman a look of mock sternness. "Stand now before the full-fledged membership of Martinis and Bikinis and make your pledge."

Angela stood first, a timid-looking creature, no bigger than a mite, as Reba might say, with translucent skin and pale green eyes. Try as she might, Joey just couldn't picture Angela doing a pole dance in pasties.

"Ladies, raise your martinis and repeat after me."

Katie and Brooke offered encouragement…by hauling Joey unceremoniously to her feet.

"All right, all right," Joey muttered. She lifted her glass of ginger ale, which Brooke had quietly asked Denver to transfer to a martini glass.

"I, state your name," Lindsay intoned.

"I, Angela Barker."

"I, state your name," Joey repeated with a smirk. Her attempt at humor got her a sharp look from Lindsay and a playful swat on the backside from Katie. She let out a sigh. "I, Joey Winfield."

"Do hereby solemnly swear on all that is served in a martini glass…"

Joey repeated the same silly words that her sisters had sworn to uphold before her. She was doing this for them, she reminded herself. And for Lindsay. For their sisterhood—which she felt she was denigrating by not sharing their mother's secret past with them.

"That once my dare is bestowed upon me, I will fulfill this most serious obligation," Lindsay continued, "and that I shall allow nothing to prevent me from my quest."

Joey and Angela finished their pledge to a round of applause and raucous cheers filled with lewd encouragement from the membership present. A full house tonight, too. Public humiliation was more Katie's style than hers. Just her luck.

"Then by the completely nonimportant, useless authority vested in me by the members of Martinis and Bikinis, as your president, I hereby declare that Joey will receive the first dare this month."

"Oh, joy," Joey muttered.

"Joey, step forward and accept your destiny."

That sounded so much more ominous to Joey than it should have. But, she stepped forward, anyway…once Brooke gave her a shove.

"Tanya, please bring forth the sacred box of dares," Lindsay said in the same ridiculous tone she'd been using since the meeting began.

Since there were so many members present tonight, the usual round table had been dispensed with in place of two rows of chairs. Tanya rose from her front-row seat and retrieved a polished wooden box from a table draped with a black velvet cloth and carried it to Lindsay. She giggled as Joey approached to take her place before Lindsay and the sacred box of dares.

"No naked skydiving," Joey told her eldest sister.

Lindsay smiled. "You will receive the dare that fate declares you were meant to receive."

Not having much faith in fate, Joey was certain she was doomed. "I mean it," Joey said sternly. "No naked skydiving." She frowned. "For at least two more weeks."

"Draw," Lindsay said with a gentle laugh.

"Do it, do it, do it," the crowd of women began to chant when Joey hesitated.

She looked to Brooke and Katie, who were chanting along with the crowd. With a deep fortifying breath, she closed her eyes, shoved her hand inside the box and felt around. Her fingers brushed against two small scrolls, each secured with a velvet tie. Both parchments were identical in size and shape. She tapped one, then the other, then finally selected the scroll closest to her.

She slipped the velvet bow from the parchment and it slowly unrolled. Silently, she read the dare and frowned, confused. There was no declaration that required her to remove her clothes. No flashing a stranger on the Green Line, no pole dancing and no naked skydiving.

"Read it," Katie called out above the din.

"The time for revealing secrets has come," Joey read. "Open your heart to the ones closest to it." She looked to Lindsay. "I don't get it."

Lindsay shrugged. "The sacred dares are meant to challenge. The universe has declared it so," she answered cryptically. "Angela Barker, step forward and embrace your destiny."

Joey rolled the parchment and secured it with the black velvet ribbon, then returned to her seat between Brooke and Katie. "I'm so disappointed," Katie said. "Talk about lightweight."

Joey shrugged, already dreading having to live up to her dare. She knew what it meant. At least to her. It meant she had no choice but to tell them about the notorious legacy left to them.

"She got the dare that was meant for her," Brooke told Katie. "Although I have to agree with Katie. You sure there's nothing on there about taking your clothes off in public?"

"Positive," Joey said. She'd have rather stripped and strolled through the office reciting the Bill of Rights. Without pasties.

"Well, first dares can be tame," Katie said. "Wasn't one of Lauren's first dares to seduce her new neighbor?"

"If you call that tame," Brooke said, "and while I don't think it's fair after what I had to do, Joey's is so obscure."

Katie shrugged. "Maybe Lindsay is right. The universe decides which dare is meant for you."

Joey took a long drink of her ginger ale. What she wanted to know was why it suddenly seemed as if the universe was out to get her.

ACCORDING TO THE RULES, Joey had one month to complete her dare. The way she figured it, that gave her thirty days to either find the right words to tell her sisters the truth about their mother, or find a way out of the dare. She supposed she could find a way to cheat, but that went so against her own personal moral code, she knew she'd never be able to pull it off.

She hit the button for the keyless entry of her car and slipped inside, firing up the engine and cranking up the heat. The mercury hovered below freezing and a light snow had started to fall. She fished her cell phone out of her purse and dialed Sebastian's cell phone while she waited for the car to warm up before driving home.

"Hello?"

The sound of his voice warmed her. "Hey, there," she said. The dread she'd been feeling since Reba's bombshell began to fade slightly.

"Where are you?"

"Freezing my ass off in my car," she said and shivered.

"You coming over?"

She wanted to, she really did. She'd love nothing more than to spend the night making love to Sebastian and forgetting everything that had happened today, but she couldn't. "I can't. I have a cat who tends to get persnickety if I leave her alone too much. You should see what she can do to a roll of toilet paper when she's mad at me. It's not pretty."

He chuckled. "I'll miss you." He lowered his voice to a low, husky rumble of sound that increased her longing.

She bit her bottom lip and tapped her gloved fingers on the steering wheel. Background noise filtered through the phone. "Where are you?"

"Why? Are we going to have phone sex now?"

She smiled. "Not exactly."

"I met up with an old buddy for a burger and a beer."

"When you're done, wanna meet me at my place?" She'd no doubt be interrogated by her grandmother if the Winfield matriarch happened to spot Sebastian's SUV parked near the carriage house overnight, but that was just too bad, she thought rebelliously. Other than Carson, she'd never brought a man back to her place for the night. Even though she and Carson had been engaged, her grandmother had still given her the standard "Winfield girls don't" lecture the one time Carson had stayed the night with her. After that particularly uncomfortable discussion, she hadn't bothered to repeat the offense.

"You sure?" Sebastian asked.

More than ever. "You want the directions or not?"

"Shoot."

She rattled off the address, but he said he'd use his GPS so she didn't bother with the actual directions to her grandparents' estate in Brookline. "Drive past the main house," she told him, "and take the side road that cuts off from the driveway. Follow that until you reach what looks like stables, but it's actually a garage. The carriage house will be on the left. You can't miss it."

"I should be there in about thirty."

"See you then," she said and disconnected the call. She tossed her cell back into her purse, then pulled away from the curb and headed toward home. Home. Where hopefully she could forget, at least for a while, that she carried the weight of the world on her shoulders.

HUNTER SIGNALED THE waitress for the check. "This is where you blow me off, isn't it? Some chippie calls and it's see ya' later, pal."

Sebastian fished his wallet from his back pocket. "I got it," he told Hunter. "And I'm not blowing you off. We're done here."

Joey was no chippie, either, but a high-class Boston Brahmin, information he chose to keep to himself for the time being. Hunter was, at best, what Sebastian would call a reverse snob. Southies didn't mess around with Beacon Hill snobs. Period.

A pair of brunettes strolled past their table wearing painted-on jeans and welcoming smiles. "I could use another beer," Hunter said, his attention zeroing in on the brunettes.

Sebastian dropped a couple of bills on the table. "No, you want to get laid."

"Nothing wrong with a little sexual diversion now and then." He leaned to the side and watched the brunettes from behind. "Now those are some nice genes."

Sebastian chuckled. "Don't you have to be on duty in the morning?"

Hunter let out an exaggerated sigh. "Yeah. And I'm getting a new partner tomorrow. Some chick who transferred from another precinct. Rumor has it she's trouble."

Hunter, a ten-year veteran of the Boston P.D., had lost his previous partner in a traffic stop gone bad three months ago. Luckily, Hunter hadn't been wounded, but Sebastian knew all too well that not all scars were physical.

"By-the-book trouble?" Sebastian asked. "Or your kind of trouble?"

Hunter shifted his attention back to Sebastian, his expression turning to granite. "Not on the job. That's not trouble, it's a nightmare."

Sebastian stood but didn't comment. A guilty

conscience, he wondered? What he and Joey were doing could turn into a nightmare, but that didn't stop him from looking forward to seeing her again. Although once she learned about his conversation with the adjuster on the *Gilson* case this afternoon, he couldn't help wonder if his nights with Joey in his bed could be numbered.

No, he thought. They were both professionals. Business was business and had nothing whatsoever to do with their personal relationship. Surely Joey would understand the difference.

"I hear she's a rat," Hunter said and stood as well.

"Who's a rat?"

"The new chick," Hunter said.

"Better keep your nose clean, then."

"Hey, you know me." Hunter shrugged into his jacket. "My nose is always clean."

Sebastian had his doubts. Not that Hunter was a bad cop or even a cop on the take—his friend was too honorable for that—but he knew for a fact Hunter had once had a thing going with one of the dispatchers.

"Some of the guys won't like having her in the house," Hunter said. "They'll make it rough for her. Which means I'll be the one she rags on."

Sebastian shrugged into his own jacket, then slapped his buddy on the shoulder. "You're tough. You can handle it."

"I guess," Hunter said. "Somebody's gotta do it. I just wish it wasn't me, you know?"

Sebastian did know, but what he didn't know was what to do about it. He considered telling Joey tonight that the client had authorized a settlement offer in the *Gilson* case, but thought better of it. Their relationship was complicated enough without him intentionally blurring the lines more than he already had.

Twenty minutes after leaving Buck's Burger and Beer Shack in South Boston, he turned onto Oak Ridge Drive in Brookline. Once again he was reminded again of the socioeconomic differences between himself and Joey. As he searched for the address she'd given him, even under the darkness of night and with the light snow falling, he could see the homes in this area were nothing short of stately.

The feminine voice of the GPS intoned he was reaching his destination. He slowed, searching for the driveway, and spied fresh tire tracks in the snow. He made the right turn and drove past an enormous Georgian brick mansion, complete with six large white columns gracing the front. He followed Joey's tire tracks to the side road she'd indicated to the carriage house, and parked his SUV next to her car.

The carriage house wasn't small by any means, although it was understated compared to the big house he'd driven past. Off to the side he could make out what he supposed was a garden in warmer months, double the size of the backyard at Hunter's folks' place where he and his friend used to play when they were kids.

He followed the flagstone path to the front door and rang the bell. As he waited for Joey to answer, he realized he couldn't possibly compete with this kind of wealth. Even reminding himself that Joey wasn't pretentious couldn't completely dispel the stab of inadequacy suddenly plaguing him.

The door swung open and his reservations evaporated at the sight of her. She still wore the same skirt she'd worn to the office, but had lost the matching jacket. Those wicked, fantasy-inspiring red heels had been replaced by a pair of thick, fuzzy blue socks.

She grabbed hold of his jacket and hauled him inside. "What took you so long?" she said and used her foot to nudge the door shut. She flung her arms around his neck and drew him down for a hot, open-mouthed kiss.

His arms automatically went around her and he pulled her close, loving the feel of her against him. Too many clothes, he thought, anxious to have her naked and beneath him.

Something rubbed against his leg, then wound

itself around his feet. And meowed. No, not a quite meow, he thought, more like a very loud yowl. He ended the kiss and looked down at his feet. "What the…?"

A golden cat with black leopardlike spots was yowling and winding itself back and forth around his calves.

Joey laughed. "Meet Molly." She stooped to pick up the feline and cuddled her to her chest. Molly purred louder than a semi truck.

"She's in a mood tonight," Joey said, "because she could see her reflection in the bottom of her food bowl by the time I got home. That's a no-no in Molly's world."

He reached out to pet the cat, who purred louder, if that were possible, and rubbed her head against his hand, in search of more affection. "At least she's friendly. My buddy's mom used to have a cat who'd run to the door and growl like a dog if anyone knocked on their door."

Joey turned and walked into the living room. Definitely a woman's domain, but not overdone, he thought, taking in the overstuffed furnishings and simple lace curtains over the leaded glass windows.

"That would be the watchdog gene," she explained and set Molly on the arm of the chair in the corner. "Molly has the grooming gene, which means don't be surprised if you wake up and she's trying to do your hair."

"Anything else I need to know?"

"She retrieves." Joey reached into a small bin beside the sofa and pulled out a bright pink twisty thing, then tossed it across the room near the fireplace. Molly zipped off the chair and bounded across the room for the toy, then promptly trotted over to him and dropped the toy at his feet.

Dubious, he bent and tossed the toy for the cat, who to his surprise, ran after it again and brought it back to him.

"Be careful," Joey warned. "Or she'll keep you doing that all night."

"How do you get her to stop?" He threw the toy again and Molly bounded after it.

"Food is always a welcome distraction."

Molly dropped the toy at his feet. He looked over at Joey, now curled up on the end of the sofa. "What now?"

"Come here, Molly," she called to the cat, but the feline wasn't interested. Not when she had a willing participant.

He scooped up the cat and the toy and carried them both to Joey. "Here," he said and sat down beside her. "You be the bad guy. She likes me."

Joey took the cat from him and cuddled her to

her chest again. "She likes you and is just trying to make a good impression," she said as she pet the cat affectionately.

He slipped his arm around Joey and pulled her, and her cat, closer. She set Molly on the floor, sans the toy, then shifted and curled her body into his. He let out a contented sigh and just sat and held Joey next to him. How many more nights like this one could they have, he wondered? A few weeks? A year? Two?

A lifetime wouldn't be enough, he realized.

"How was your girls' night out?" he asked, needing to seriously derail the direction his thoughts had taken. He wasn't a lifetime kind of guy, or so he'd been told. Or had he just been involved with the wrong women? Unlike the last woman he'd been relatively serious about, Joey understood the demands of his job. But would that turn out be more of a liability than an asset?

She rested her head on his shoulder. "Strange," she said. "I officially joined Martinis and Bikinis tonight."

"You drink martinis wearing a bikini?"

She laughed and the sound chased away the last of the cold night that had been clinging to him. "No," she said, then explained about the women's social club she and her sisters had joined, run by her half-sister Lindsay.

"It's all about feeling empowered by accepting

dares that challenge yourself. I drew my first dare tonight," she said and explained some of the more daring adventures the women of the club had completed.

"You don't have to dance naked in the Common do you?"

"No. My dare won't even get my half-naked body on the front page of the local tattler like it did poor Brookie."

He remembered hearing about something in the paper recently, a scandal about David Carerra and an unnamed Boston socialite. He looked down at Joey. "Sox Sex Scandal? *That* was your sister?"

Joey nodded and laughed. "It really wasn't her fault. She didn't realize that pasties required paste to stay in place."

"What do you have to do?" he asked. He didn't care if it was chauvinistic. He was damn certain he didn't want Joey parading around Boston in the nude.

"Nothing quite so scandalous," she said, but there was an edge to her voice that still concerned him.

"Can you talk about it, or are you sworn to secrecy?"

She tipped her head back to look at him. The hint of a frown marred her forehead. "I suppose I could," she said slowly. "I only swore to uphold my promise to embrace my destiny, or some such thing."

"So?"

"The time for revealing secrets has come," Joey said as if she were reciting from memory. "Open your heart to the ones closest to it."

"Do you have a secret you want to tell me?"

Her blue eyes darkened ever so slightly. She reached up and cupped his cheek in her small, warm palm. "Are you the one closest to my heart, Sebastian?" she whispered.

He hadn't meant for things between them to become serious, at least not this soon. Hell, they'd only known each other a week. How ridiculous was that? But, he thought, when something was right, it was right, and he didn't think anything could be more right than how he felt about Joey. He'd be a fool not to recognize what was directly in front of him.

Turning his face, he kissed her palm. "Would you like me to be?" he asked her.

Emotion filled her gaze as she looked at him. "I think I would. Very much."

13

SEBASTIAN WASN'T CLOSE to her heart, he was in it, Joey thought as she shifted slightly on the bed to accommodate his body next to hers. In fact, she'd swear he'd moved right in and took up residence, right there in her heart acting as if he owned the place, where she'd least expected to find him. Love had been the last thing she'd been looking for, but heaven help her, she didn't think she had enough strength to evict him.

It wasn't an actual declaration of love, she reminded herself as he dipped his head and kissed her. Just dangerously close enough to make her feel open and exposed.

A part of her wanted to take the words back, yet she instinctively knew Sebastian would never intentionally hurt her. With him, she felt something she'd never experienced before with the opposite sex. She felt safe. Safe in the knowledge that with him, her heart would be a tender commodity, a gift to be treasured.

There'd be time for revealing secrets later. Right now she wanted to experience the delightful sensations coursing through her as Sebastian trailed little biting kisses down her throat and along her jaw while he gently kneaded her breast in his hand. With his thumb, he teased her nipples into tight buds. She arched her back, and wound her arms around his neck, urging him to take her breast into the heat of his mouth.

Joey sighed as spirals of pleasure rippled over her skin when he nipped at her lip, then soothed the spot with his tongue before taking her mouth in another hot, deep kiss. She'd never get enough of this man. And maybe, she thought, that wasn't such a bad deal, after all.

She tasted him, loved him with her mouth as the sensual fire between them sparked, ignited and burned hot. Without breaking the kiss, he pulled her beneath him and she welcomed him between her legs, rolling her hips up to meet his. The ridge of his arousal wedged intimately against her heated center, sending intoxicating spirals of heat over her skin.

His mouth left hers to suckle her breast. He teased and laved her nipple until she moaned from the intense desire building up inside her. What was left of her defenses shattered. She'd never dreamed she could want a man as much as she wanted Sebastian in this very moment. He held more than her breast in his hand…he held her heart.

Was Sebastian what fate had in mind for her? Did she have enough faith to believe in the emotions crowding her heart?

She was a fool for falling in love with him. Even though she'd known from the minute she'd met him such a phenomenon was possible, she hadn't really expected it to happen to her. How was it possible that with so little effort, Sebastian had managed to strip her down to her most basic self, to that place where she exposed her heart and soul to him?

He shifted, the weight of his body sliding down the length of hers. Using his tongue, he created a fire that continued to burn hot, one she never wanted extinguished. She wanted him to fan those flames until they were both scorched by the power of not only their lovemaking, but also their emotions. Until there was no turning back, for either of them.

She wanted earth-shattering, and he delivered, using his hands and mouth to bring her to an orgasm so powerful she wept. Beneath him, she lay vulnerable, almost defenseless emotionally. Tonight, with Sebastian, the only secret she held was the three little words that felt too new to be spoken aloud.

Before her racing heart could calm, he moved over her, entering her with one deep, hard thrust.

She welcomed him and the pure pleasure of their joining. She held him close and kissed him, tasting herself on his tongue. Her movements equaled his, until he cupped her bottom in his hands and lifted her, burying himself inside her.

Their lovemaking became wild. Desire pulled at her desperately, her body demanding fulfillment. With her legs wrapped tightly around his waist, she pulled him deeper inside. Her body practically vibrated from the force of their passion as their bodies met and parted with increasing urgency. Each thrust of Sebastian's body pushed her closer to the edge until she slipped over the side where her world shattered into a million tiny pinpoints of vibrant light and exquisite sensation. A heartbeat later, he followed her into sweet oblivion.

Together they lay, breast to chest, both of them breathing hard as their hearts beat heavily in perfect rhythm. With his face buried in the crook of her neck, he kissed her throat. Their bodies still intimately joined, he rose up on his elbows and looked down at her. The tenderness in his dark gaze made her heart ache.

Gently, he brushed the moist tendrils of hair from her face. "This has gone somewhere we never planned," he said, his voice rough.

"I know," she whispered, then pulled him down for a long, slow kiss. The words could come later.

SHE'D BEEN SUMMONED. Sebastian hadn't been gone ten minutes this morning when her phone had rung. It'd been Louise, the Winfield's longtime house-keeper, with a message. If she would be so kind as to please stop in and see her grandmother before going into the city today.

As if she didn't have enough on her mind, now she had to endure one of Grandmother's lectures about the proper deportment of Winfield girls. If she heard the word *shameful* just once, she'd…she frowned at herself in the full-length mirror. She'd what? Spit in Granny's eye?

"Yeah, right." She gave the hem of her cream-colored mock-neck sweater a tug, then eyed her skirt, another longish wool plaid, this one in the colors of autumn, in deference to the snowy day. She looked more like a coed than a lawyer. Oh, well. She didn't have time to change.

Molly lay curled on the chaise. She lifted her head long enough to meow at Joey, as if to say, "Sure you will."

"Why not?" she said to the cat as she dropped down on the chaise to pull on a pair of chocolate-brown boots. "I have enough trailer trash in the family tree. I could pull it off if I really wanted to, you know."

Molly yawned and went back to napping, obviously not interested.

Joey left the chaise and crossed the bedroom to her dresser. She opened her jewelry box and fished out the heart-shaped gold locket her mother had given her when she'd graduated from high school, along with her favorite pair of gold earrings, a cute little dangly, twisted pair of three small hoops, subtle enough to wear to the office. After slipping into a dark brown wool blazer, she checked that Molly had plenty of fresh food and water, then left the carriage house.

It took her a few more minutes than she'd anticipated to reach the main house. She'd left her car out last night for Sebastian's benefit, and had had to sweep the snow off before driving the short distance.

Joey found her grandmother alone in the dining room, seated at one end of the ridiculously long table. She approached and bent to dutifully kiss her grandmother's cheek. "Good morning, Grandmother."

"Good morning, dear," Evelyn Winfield said pleasantly. "Would you like some breakfast?"

Joey took in the plate of dry whole wheat toast, the small bowl of fresh citrus and cup of weak tea in front of her grandmother. A sesame bagel and a vanilla latte from her favorite coffee house across the street from the office were more her speed this morning. She desperately needed the extra caffeine, considering she hadn't had more than three or four hours sleep.

"No, thank you," she said, then pulled out a chair and sat at the table. "You wanted to see me?"

"You know there is a family dinner scheduled for this coming Sunday," her grandmother said.

"Yes, ma'am."

She cast those blue eyes at Joey, the same shade Joey saw when she looked at herself every morning in the mirror, the same that had belonged to her father. For the first time, she was struck by how old her grandmother suddenly appeared.

"This business with Brooke," Evelyn said. "It's gone on long enough, don't you agree?"

By "long enough," Joey assumed she meant the fact that Brooke hadn't made an appearance at a family dinner since the night she drove off on the back of David's motorcycle. "Have you spoken to her?" Joey asked, even though she knew Brooke and their grandmother hadn't spoken in almost two months.

Evelyn cast her gaze downward, but not before Joey caught a glimpse of anguish in her grand-mother's eyes. "I know you girls are close. I was

hoping you would speak to her on our behalf."
Meaning her and the Admiral.

Joey reached across the table and gently settled
her hand over her grandmother's. Evelyn appeared
startled by the contact, but that didn't deter Joey. "I
think it'd be best if you spoke with her yourself,
Grandmother."

The look Evelyn gave her was as sharp as cut
crystal. "I shouldn't have to invite her." Her chilled
tone matched the expression in her eyes. "She
knows she's welcome here. She's a Winfield."

"Yes," Joey said. "She is. But I still think you
should be the one to call her."

Evelyn snatched her hand away. "Very well," she
said, then dismissed the subject by picking up her
teacup and taking a quiet sip.

Joey stood and walked to the sideboard. She
opened the drawer, withdrew a pad and pen and
carefully wrote down a telephone number. "While
you're at it—" she set the paper on the gleaming
surface for her grandmother to see "—you should
call and invite Lindsay, too."

Her grandmother appeared startled by the sug-
gestion. "But, she's not a Winfield."

"No, she isn't. But she is our mother's daughter."

"I don't see why..." Evelyn started, then
promptly closed her mouth.

"She's our sister, Grandmother," Joey said firmly. "That should be enough."

As Joey expected, her grandmother remained stubbornly silent on the subject. When Evelyn picked up a slice of toast and carefully smoothed a minuscule amount of butter on one corner, Joey decided the conversation had come to an end.

Better get out while the going is good, she thought, anxious to escape before her luck changed. She'd fully expected a stern lecture from her grandmother this morning for having a man staying the night. It didn't matter that she was a grown woman. Those were just details when it came to the proper behavior of a Winfield girl.

"I need to get to the office," she said, then turned to leave. She'd been inches from a clean getaway when her grandmother's voice stopped her.

"Josephine…?"

Joey cringed. Damn. She'd been so close. She pasted a smile on her face and looked over her shoulder. "Yes, Grandmother?" she asked, hopefully conveying just the right level of innocence.

"I'll expect to see your young man at dinner Sunday." Evelyn's tone and expression were stern. "Is that understood?"

Joey let out a sigh. "Yes, ma'am."

"Very well."

Yes, Joey thought, very well indeed. For whom she hadn't yet decided. Certainly not her, or Sebastian.

Poor guy, she thought as she slipped out through the kitchen to the back door. She wondered how he'd hold up under what would be nothing less than an interrogation—Winfield style, of course.

"YOU'RE KIDDING, RIGHT?"

"Nope. Family dinner. Sunday night. Be there or be square, mister." Joey kept her voice low enough so they wouldn't be overheard. She probably should have waited until they'd left the office to dump this on him, but it was after hours. The support staff had cleared out over an hour ago and only a small handful of attorneys remained in the office. But still, she probably should've waited. Wasn't she the one always preaching about keeping their private life private?

She flipped the code book she'd been reviewing closed and reached her arms over her head to stretch the kinks from her back. She'd spent the entire afternoon researching case law in hopes of unearthing an applicable precedent to use in her response to a motion to suppress evidence she'd received in the mail that morning from plaintiff's counsel in the *Gilson* matter.

Preston Thomas was asserting that his client's

sexual history wasn't relevant to the case. Joey held a different opinion. The fact that Patricia Gilson hadn't been faithful in her marriage should be considered by a jury. A fact that certainly didn't excuse her deceased husband's philandering, but at least helped paint a better picture of the defendant. Natasha Pierce wasn't quite the evil, husband-stealing witch the plaintiff wanted the jury to believe.

Sebastian sat in the chair opposite Joey's desk, a thick file balanced in his lap. She tried to catch a glimpse, but the file was upside down, preventing her from reading the label.

A deep frown pulled his eyebrows together. "Why?" he asked.

"We have them once a month. It's a Winfield tradition," she said. "Look, it won't be so bad. Liam's survived several. And David certainly held his own with my family. You have nothing to worry about."

He shot her a dubious look. "Do I have to decide right this minute?"

She flashed him a smile. "There's nothing to decide. It was clearly a summons. I was specifically *ordered* to bring you to dinner." Her gaze slipped pointedly to the file in his lap. "What's that? New case?"

"I assigned you two new cases this week already."

"Yes, but you took three away," she reminded him.

"And I warned all of the associates there would be some shuffling of cases."

She detected a hint of defensiveness in his tone. "I know," she said and leaned back in her chair, giving him a flashy grin. "Didn't you get my memo about *Marshall v. Collins?* I settled it this morning, so I really could use a new case file. Have we gotten any of those new med mal cases yet? I'd really love to work one of those."

He didn't smile in return as she'd hoped he would. "Actually," he said, "you had another one of your cases settled today, too."

She frowned as she tried to think if she had any other cases where she'd made a settlement offer, and came up blank. "Really? Which one?"

He leaned forward and set the file he'd been holding on the desk. "This one."

Her gaze dipped to the label, and her frown deepened. "I didn't make a settlement offer on *Gilson,*" she said, lifting her gaze to his.

"I know," he said. "I did."

She couldn't have heard him right. He knew how important *Gilson* was to her. Why would he go behind her back? Just to prove to the senior partners he was the boss?

She tapped her pen impatiently on the desk. "When did this happen?"

"Yesterday," he said. "I reviewed the case and decided taking it to trial would've been a mistake."

"*You* decided?" She hadn't meant for it to sound like an accusation, but she couldn't help herself. *Gilson* was her case, dammit.

"It's my job, Joey."

Frustrated, she tossed her pen on the desk. It skittered across the surface and slid to the floor at Sebastian's feet. "You should've at least discussed it with me first."

His expression turned dark. "When was I supposed to do that? When you were having a minor meltdown you wouldn't tell me about? Or while I was stuck in a deposition all day?"

She gave him a cold stare right back. "You could've told me last night."

"When would you have preferred? Before or after we made love?"

If he'd slapped her, she couldn't have been more stunned. "I can't believe you just said that."

"I can't believe you're turning this into something personal."

She crossed her arms over her chest. "Oh, and you're not?"

"No. It's business, Joey. I talked with the adjuster yesterday afternoon and convinced him to offer the policy limits to the plaintiff. After a discussion with plaintiff's counsel, he agreed to talk with his client. I had a call back within the hour that she'd accepted our offer."

"No, it is personal." She came out of her chair and slapped her palms on the desk. "You didn't even bother to meet with the defendant. You had your mind made up about her the minute you heard what the case was about."

Abruptly, he stood. "The hell I did."

"Oh? No," she argued heatedly. "You most certainly did. Natasha Pierce is the other woman, so in your mind, she's the one at fault here. She lured Gilson, like she's some evil seductress. If he hadn't been screwing her, he might still be alive."

"I never said that."

"You didn't have to. You made your position perfectly clear."

"Now wait a minute—"

"No, you wait," she fired back at him. "You don't know what happened between Natasha Pierce and Frederick Gilson. You don't know what kind of marriage he had with Patricia Gilson. But because Natasha Pierce is the other woman, she's as good as guilty in your opinion."

"It would have been the jury's opinion, too."

She shoved off the desk. "You don't know that," she said, her voice rising.

"And you do?" he roared back.

"Did you ever stop to think that maybe Gilson and Pierce were in love? That his marriage was over long before he ever started seeing her? The plaintiff might have been hurt, but that doesn't mean it's our client's fault."

"You're condoning *his* actions?"

And then it struck her. Yes, he was making a moral judgment, of that she had little doubt. But his actions went so much deeper. "No, Sebastian," she said lowering her voice. "I'm not. But sometimes people have reasons for the things they do. Reasons only they understand, or that make sense to them."

Like her mother. Or maybe even her Grandmother Breckenridge. She hadn't been there. She didn't know why they'd chosen their particular paths, but she had to believe they'd done what they had because it had made sense to them at the time. Right or wrong, who was she to judge them?

"They're not all selfish bastards," she said quietly. "They're not all like Emerson Stanhope." Or Nathan Sprecht, the man who'd fathered Lindsay and Brooke, then abandoned her mother.

Sebastian's expression turned to granite, his gaze glacial. The phone on Joey's desk rang and she picked it up before it could ring a second time.

"Yes?" Her heart sank when she heard the voice

of Barbara Johnson, the woman who ran the halfway house. One of the girls was in trouble. Could she help?

"I'm on my way," she told Barb and hung up the phone. She looked at Sebastian. "I have to go. Will I see you Sunday?"

The look he gave her was hardly encouraging. "What do you think?" he said stonily, then turned and stormed out of her office.

She took that as a resounding *when hell freezes over.*

14

A LITTLE BEFORE eleven-thirty on Saturday morning, after ringing the bell and not getting an answer, Joey used her old house key to let herself into her parents' home on Hawthorn Drive where Brooke still lived. Brooke knew she was coming, she'd called both of her sisters last night asking them to meet her here at noon today, so she was mildly concerned that her sister wasn't there to greet her.

It'd been close to midnight when she'd finally gotten home last night. One of the girls from the halfway house had been arrested on a possible parole violation, all because of the company she'd kept. Carla Brendell's so-called boyfriend had been hauled in on suspicion of being involved in a string of home invasion robberies that had taken place in South Boston over the past two weeks. Because Carla had been with the jerk at the time he'd been taken in to custody, the arresting officer had taken her in for violating the conditions of her parole, after running a wants and warrants check and discovering she was a parolee in the presence of a suspected criminal.

After some fast talking on Joey's part with the district attorney, he'd finally agreed to release Carla back to the halfway house. Carla's legal troubles hadn't gone away. Monday afternoon she'd have to appear before the local magistrate, but at least she hadn't had to spend the weekend behind bars.

Joey dropped her coat and bag on the chair in the foyer, then walked into the kitchen in search of her sister. A note from Brooke was tacked to the refrigerator with a magnet that resembled a book cover, indicating she'd run to the market and would be back before noon. Katie wasn't due to arrive for another thirty minutes, but knowing her younger sister, Joey figured she'd show up an hour late.

She hadn't heard from Sebastian since he'd stormed out of her office last night. There'd been no messages waiting for her when she'd gotten home from dealing with the mess with Carla, and no voice mail or text messages had been sent to her cell. Not that she blamed him for his silence. She hadn't exactly fought fair. But then, in her opinion, neither had he when it came to the way he'd gone behind her back on the *Gilson* matter.

She supposed she did owe him an apology.

Having all that spare time on her hands last night at the police precinct in South Boston, she'd been able to replay their argument. She couldn't admit she was totally in the wrong. In her opinion, they were equally responsible, but it didn't matter. She'd rather be with Sebastian than be right.

She filled the teakettle and set it on the stove, then left the kitchen. In the front parlor, she stopped to admire Brooke's fish aquarium. "Hi, fishies," she said, and lightly tapped the glass, smiling when one of the more colorful fish—a parrot cichlid, she believed Brooke had said it was—swam up to the glass as if in greeting. She dragged her finger back and forth across the glass, laughing when the fish followed her movements. "Who says fish are boring?"

She tucked her hands in the back pockets of her jeans and watched the fish swim away. She loved this house, and loved that Brooke hadn't made any sweeping changes. She would eventually, Joey knew, but for now she chose to enjoy the familiarity of it all. Practically every memory she had of her youth took place here. But what she loved the most was that she could still feel her mother's presence, especially in Mother's bedroom.

She left the parlor and climbed the stairs to the second level. Other than having cleared out most of their mother's clothing items, Brooke hadn't changed her room. Every wall, including the ceiling, was still papered in a busy pattern of yellow lilies on a blue background. The dark wood furnishings were a bit more masculine, but the room definitely had her mother's stamp on it.

She pulled in a deep breath, smiling when she caught the light, lingering scent of her mother's favorite perfume. Walking to the bed, she sat on the edge and drew her hand over one of the floral print throw pillows edged in lace. The room had been decorated with a feminine hand, but she recalled that her father hadn't seemed to mind. That he'd loved her mother, and she him, was never in doubt.

So many fond memories, yet sad ones, too. Like the time she'd found her mother sitting on the bed, hugging a pillow to her chest, her face stained with tears. It hadn't been quite a year after John Winfield had passed unexpectedly. Joey had asked her mother what was wrong. Her mother had managed a watery smile and simply said, "I was just talking to your father."

Joey had automatically assumed the tears were because her mother missed her husband, but then she'd explained she'd been crying because she could no longer hear his voice. She could recall his words, but the exact timbre of his voice had begun to fade from her memory.

Joey had hugged her mother and together they'd cried. Six months later they'd wept again, when Daisy Winfield had been diagnosed with pancreatic cancer.

Joey swiped at the tears blurring her vision now. "I get it, Mom," she whispered into the empty room. Her mother had been so in love with her husband, a part of her had given up when she'd lost him. Joey had always suspected as much, but now, standing in this room where her parents had loved, where they'd argued, where they'd laughed and planned and lived, and sadly, where both of them had passed on, she finally understood the power of the kind of love her parents had shared.

Joey flicked at the lace edge of the pillow with her finger. She knew it made little sense, but then she'd also come to understand that love rarely did. Love wasn't logical or pragmatic. It was, as her mother would have said, what it was.

She let out a sigh and accepted the truth—that she, without a doubt, was in love with Sebastian Stanhope.

Even though he was angry with her at the moment, she didn't doubt that he loved her, too. She might not have said the words to him yet, but she felt them in her heart. Only it was no longer enough. She had to tell him.

"What are you doing in here?"

Joey started at the accusatory note in Katie's voice. "Just needing to feel a little closer to Mom," she said. "You're early."

"Don't get used to it. It's a fluke." Kate stepped more fully in the room. "I do the same thing, you know," she said and sat on the bed beside Joey.

"What's that?"

"Come here to feel a little closer to Mom," Katie said. "I didn't expect to find anyone in here."

"Where is everyone?" came Brooke's voice from downstairs.

"Up here," Joey called out to Brooke. "In Mom's room."

A few moments later, Brooke stood in the doorway. Her cheeks were flushed from the cold, giving her skin a soft glow. She wore a pair of sensible khakis, but her sweater was far from her usual oversized style. Instead, she wore a soft blue understated cashmere that accentuated her slender curves. Who knew? Brookie had a bod.

"I made the tea," Brooke said. "And I bought fresh croissants and some chicken salad for lunch. Shall we go downstairs?"

Joey thought about that for a moment and finally shook her head. "Can it wait?" she asked. "It's right that we talk in here."

She felt her mother's presence in this room, as if Daisy were giving her approval to Joey for the secrets she was about to reveal to her sisters. Maybe it wasn't fate that had a hand in the dare she'd drawn at Chassy the other night, she thought. Maybe it was something else, something inexplicable, but so right.

A slight frown marred Katie's perfect complexion. "What's going on?" she asked Joey. "What was so important that we had to meet here?"

"Yes, that's what I'd like to know." Brooke crossed the room and sat in their father's wing chair by the window. "Did you get one of those early detection pregnancy tests?"

Katie's eyes widened. "Pregnant?"

One of Brooke's eyebrows winged skyward. "She and Sebastian had unprotected sex."

Katie's mouth fell open in shock as she stared at Joey. "And to think *you* were the one who gave me a supply of condoms and showed me how to use them when I went off to college," she said once she recovered from her initial surprise. "Geez, Joey. What are you? Sixteen?"

"No," Joey said, sounding very much like a sixteen-year-old. She stood and walked to her mother's bureau. She opened a drawer, but it was empty. "It just…happened."

"Are we really going to be aunties?" Katie asked with a distinct note of excitement edging her voice. "And don't worry. We won't be anything like Great Aunt Jo. We'll spoil her rotten. Not a single deportment lecture. We promise. Don't we, Brooke?"

"Absolutely," Brooke confirmed.

Joey smiled as she turned to face her sisters. "If you are going to be aunties, you'll be the first to know. Well," she added with a private smile, "after Sebastian, that is."

"How does he feel about the possibility?" Brooke asked her.

She let out a sigh and rested her backside against the bureau. "We're not speaking at the moment."

Katie kicked off her shoes and climbed onto the middle of the bed. She hugged a pillow to her chest, reminding Joey of their mother. "That's not an answer," Katie said.

"What happened?" Brooke wanted to know.

"Long story short, I overreacted."

"Oh, like that's a big surprise," chided Katie. "You can get so pissy sometimes."

"Are you going to tell us what the argument was about?" Brooke asked her.

"Just something at work." Something that should've been business, but she'd gotten her panties into a twist and let it get personal. "It's not important."

"Important enough for you not to be speaking to each other," Brooke said sagely.

"We'll work it out," Joey told them, and hoped she was right.

Okay, Joey thought. No more hesitating. "I appreciate the moral support, but that's not why I asked you both to meet me here today." She pulled in a quick, fortifying breath. "I had lunch with Reba day before yesterday."

"How is she?" Katie asked, instantly concerned.

"Good. We talked about Mom."

"Yes," Brooke said. "We often do as well. She misses her."

"We all do," Katie said.

"We talked about Mom," Joey said again, "about her past, specifically." At her sisters' confused expressions, she told them of the invitation addressed to their mother she'd found at Reba's.

"An invitation to what?" Katie asked.

"A reunion," Joey told them. "It was from Elegance Escort Service. Apparently Mom was once employed by them."

Katie frowned. Brooke concentrated on plucking at a nonexistent piece of fuzz on the hem of her sweater.

Katie was the first to speak. "When you say 'escort service,'" she asked cautiously, "you don't mean that Mom…?"

"She was a paid escort, Katie," Joey explained. "She went on dates with men who paid a fee."

Her little sister nodded slowly, carefully digesting the information. So far, they were both taking the news so much better than she had. She'd nearly come unglued.

"Why was the invitation sent to Reba?" Brooke asked.

"Because she and Mom both worked for this agency. I guess Mom didn't exactly want to leave a forwarding address when she married Dad."

"But she didn't…" Anguish filled Katie's expressive gaze. "I mean, she wasn't…God, I can't even say it."

"A prostitute?" Brooke filled in the blank with a slight edge to her voice.

"No," Joey said firmly. "But, uh…our Grandmother Breckenridge apparently *was* a member of the world's oldest profession."

Even staid Brooke appeared shocked at that bit of tarnished news. "You're kidding."

Joey caught her bottom lip between her teeth and slowly shook her head. She'd especially worried how Brooke would take the news. Brooke had already felt the sting of discovering she wasn't a Winfield by blood. This news could end up separating her even further from her family, and that was not something Joey wanted to see happen. Still, they had a right to know about their legacy, regardless of how notorious or unseemly.

However inappropriate, Katie giggled. "God, can you imagine what would happen if Great Aunt Jo heard this one? She'd have a stroke for sure."

Brooke's gaze hardened. "It's none of her business. Or anyone's for that matter."

"I agree," said Joey. "Especially Evil-Lyn. She's the last person I want hearing of this."

"No wonder Mom never wanted to talk about her past," Brooke said. "I always wondered. I never understood, but I guess now I do."

"So," Katie asked, hugging the pillow tighter, "how exactly did it all happen? How did Mom end up an escort of all things."

Joey returned to the bed and sat where she could see both Katie and Brooke. "It's not like Mom aspired to be an escort," Joey said. "Reba told me they were living in Providence at the time. Mom was barely seventeen and had nowhere to go. The night she met Reba, she was sitting in an all-night diner because she had no other place to go. Reba didn't state specifically, but I got the impression they both were on the verge of turning a few tricks themselves as a matter of survival."

"How horrible for Mom," Brooke said. "No wonder she put up with all the crap Aunt Jo gave her when she first married Dad. It kinda makes sense now when you think about it. The lesser of two evils."

Joey agreed, and said so.

"Where was this Grandma? Too busy turning tricks to care for her own daughter?" The censure in Katie's tone wasn't surprising, given the circumstances.

"Reba wasn't too clear on that part of it," Joey said with a shrug. "I don't know if the passage of time has dimmed her memory, or she didn't want us to know. It's probably safe to assume she was no longer in the picture for whatever reason, seeing as Mom was homeless when she met Reba."

"Do you think she's still alive?" Brooke asked.

"Probably not," Joey surmised.

"But how did Mom and Reba get from Providence to Boston? How did they become…you know?"

"Escorts, Katie," Joey said a bit snappishly. "It's not a dirty word. You can say it. Not all escort services are run by Mayflower Madams."

"I didn't mean—"

Joey let out a sigh. "I know. I'm sorry."

At Katie's nod, Joey continued. "Reba told me

she and Mom met a Janice Neely one night when they were hanging out at the bus station in Providence. She supposedly overheard Mom and Reba talking, one thing led to another and Janice told them about the escort service."

"God, what do you think they were doing at the bus station?" Brooke asked.

"Let's just assume it was a place to get out of the cold," Joey answered. "Anyway, this Neely woman offered them a roof over their heads, regular meals and a safe way to earn a living that didn't include selling their bodies for a couple of bucks in a bus station. According to Reba, she and Mom were a couple of poor kids with no prospects in sight, and Janice Neely was offering them a dream come true. A home, a hot meal and they could hold on to their dignity."

"Was it?" Brooke asked. "Mom never talked about any of this."

"It couldn't have been all that bad," Katie said. "Remember that picture we found of Mom? She didn't exactly look miserable."

"Reba said Mom never wanted us to know," Joey told them. "Can you blame her? This isn't exactly the stuff of bedtime stories. But she swears Mom never took money for sex, if that's what you're asking."

"But our grandmother did," Brooke said, her tone filled with censure.

Joey looked at her sister. "You know what I think? I think she wasn't much of a mother to our mom. That makes her even less of a grandmother to me."

"Good point," Katie agreed. "Although it does make for a pretty damn shocking skeleton falling out of the closet."

"There's something else," Joey said. "I don't know if we should tell Lindsay. I'm not sure how she'd take something like this."

"I'm still reeling," Katie admitted. "I can't imagine how Lindsay would react."

"I thought about asking her here today," Joey said, "but I just wasn't sure so I decided against it. Brooke, you're closer to her than Katie or I. If we decide to tell her, maybe you should be the one to do it."

"I wouldn't exactly call us close," Brooke said thoughtfully. "She is coming around."

"She's a lot more receptive to us than when she first sent us those invitations to join Martinis and Bikinis," Katie said, then looked to Brooke. "What do you think?"

"She is family," Joey added. "She has a right to know, I just don't know if now is the right time to tell her."

"No, Joey's right," Brooke finally said. "She is our sister and we share a blood bond, but one thing we'll never share is our history."

"What are you talking about?" Katie asked. "Thanks to Mom, we have one hell of a colorful history."

"That's Mom's history," Brooke explained. "I'm referring to *our* history. No matter how welcome we make Lindsay feel, there'll always be something missing because we weren't raised together."

"Brooke's right," Joey added. She looked fondly at her little sister. "We can tell Lindsay all the stories we want about our childhood, but she wasn't a part of it. To her, it'll always be just stories. Nothing can ever change that."

Katie angrily tossed the pillow aside. "Sometimes I get really mad at Mom for doing what she did. Why couldn't she have just kept Lindsay?"

"It was a different time then, Katie," Brooke told her. "It couldn't have been easy for her."

Katie looked to Joey, who nodded in agreement. "I think Mom had a lot more courage than you're giving her credit for," Joey said. "Can you imagine for one minute what it must have been like for her giving away a child? Based on the things we've found, it's obvious Mom never forgot about Lindsay."

"Okay, so I'm a shit for thinking that way." Katie scooted off the bed. "But so you both know, I don't always feel that way. Just sometimes."

"That's okay," Brooke said and stood. She

crossed the room and slung her arm over Katie's shoulder. "Sometimes I get a little angry, too."

Katie let out a sigh and offered up a wan smile. "Some legacy she left us, huh?" She looked over at Joey, still seated on the bed. "I guess we just have to deal with it."

"It doesn't change the fact that Mom loved us," Joey told Katie.

"I know," Katie said. "Can we have lunch now? I'm starved."

"Good idea," Brooke said and then looked to Joey. "So, what are you going to do to make things right with Sebastian? Grovel?"

Joey grinned and came off the bed. "If necessary," she said, and meant it. As her sisters could attest, she never had been very good at groveling, but she'd give it a shot if it meant patching things up with Sebastian. She still hadn't figured out what to do about their work situation, but she decided to play it by ear for the time being.

Brooke turned to leave, but Katie rushed over to the closet. She opened the door and peered inside. "All's clear," she said cheerfully.

"What are you doing?" Joey asked her.

Katie grinned. "Making sure there aren't any more skeletons hiding in there. We've had enough, don't you think?"

15

JOEY COMMITTED AN unpardonable sin—she was twenty minutes late for cocktails. She'd waited until the last possible minute, then waited another fifteen before finally giving up hope that Sebastian would show.

What do you think?

Apparently she'd been right in assuming he'd meant no way in hell would he subject himself to a Winfield family dinner. Or more accurately, it'd be a cold day in hell before subjecting himself to her presence again. Did that mean she would also be correct in assuming all that they'd really had was nothing more than a week-long, one-night stand?

As much as it hurt to do so, she couldn't ignore the truth. Sebastian's silence all weekend spoke volumes.

Working together would be uncomfortable, but she'd be damned if she'd give up her position at the firm just because she'd been stupid and had a reckless, albeit brief, affair with her boss. She didn't want to believe it really could be over after one silly argument that never should've happened. But since she hadn't heard from him all weekend, what other conclusion could she possibly draw?

Yeah, and what if you are pregnant? What then?

She tugged her long wool dress coat a little tighter around her and tried not to think about it. She'd have the answer to that all-important question in about ten days. Until then, she was going to take Brooke's advice and try not to worry until she had something to actually worry about.

A brisk wind kicked up, so she quickened her pace and hurriedly walked across the grounds of the estate to the main house. Instead of using the back door to slip in through the kitchen, as was her habit, she walked toward the front of the elegant Georgian brick mansion to the front door. If she was going in alone, then dammit, she'd do it with her head held high, not slinking in through the service entrance as if she had something to hide.

Like a broken heart.

She'd known it would happen. That first night with Sebastian, she'd seen the writing on the sheets. Tall, dark and a sense of humor. Her favorite combination. But even knowing she'd end up with broken heart hadn't stopped her. She loved the man. Now she had to deal with it. She only wished it didn't hurt so much.

As she rounded the low trimmed evergreen shrubs, she came upon the brick parking court. The safety lights turned on as she passed the motion detector, and she skimmed her gaze along the row of vehicles parked there.

The usual suspects were all in attendance, including her Great Aunt Josephine and cousin Eve. She didn't see Brooke's car, but there was a spiffy-looking Ferrari she believed belonged to David.

Joey managed a smile. Brooke hadn't said a word to her yesterday about coming to dinner tonight, so she had no idea when her sister had even spoken to Grandmother. She was just glad to see that her grandmother had taken the first step in repairing the rift between them. Lindsay's car, however, remained noticeably absent.

Oh well, she thought. One pride-swallowing moment at a time.

She stopped, spying a large silver SUV parked at the end of the row. She couldn't miss it. Those Florida plates stuck out like a sore thumb amid all the Massachusetts plates. Her heart skipped a definite, hopeful beat.

"Oh my God," she muttered and picked up her pace. She couldn't believe Sebastian would willingly walk into the lion's den alone. Good heavens, she could only imagine the interrogation her family was putting him through without her to run interference.

"Joey!"

She stopped abruptly and turned at the sound of Sebastian's voice, chiding herself for the ridiculous sense of relief coursing through her. He shut the door to the SUV and started toward her.

Like a dummy, her heart took off like a rocket at the sight of him striding toward her. He didn't look as if he'd shown up just to dump her, so she took that as a positive sign. In fact, he looked positively delicious. Beneath a cashmere blend coat, he wore a dark navy suit, pristine white shirt and a patterned tie in subdued hues. Even his shoes were highly polished.

"Why didn't you come to the carriage house?" she asked when he approached. Certainly not much of a greeting, and not exactly what she'd planned to say when she saw him, either. "I'm sorry" being at the top of her list, quickly followed by "I love you."

"I was running late, so I figured you'd already be at the house," he said. "Joey, listen. I'm—"

"No." She lifted her hand and covered his lips with her gloved fingers. "I'm the one who owes you an apology. I wanted to take *Gilson* to trial and I overreacted. I made it personal and that was wrong. What can I say?" she added with a shrug.

"Katie's always accusing me of being pissy. I guess my inner bitch really is alive and well."

The chilling wind blew her hair into her face. She pushed it away and looked up at him. His expression remained bland, and that made her nervous.

"I never should've said what I did," she continued in a rush. She was starting to ramble, but anything was better than silence. "That crack about Emerson was uncalled for, Sebastian. I'm sorry."

He shook his head slightly. Her heart took a nosedive. "It's no longer important," he said.

She frowned. *Why?* she almost demanded. But for once in her life, she kept her big trap shut. She refused to jump to conclusions.

Still, she couldn't help but feel more than a wee bit nervous. Why wasn't it important, she wanted to know? Because he no longer cared? About her? About them?

Oh, hell.

"Why isn't it important?" she asked anyway. Apparently she was hopeless.

"Can we just go inside?" he asked. He rubbed his big hands together. "It's below freezing out here."

She shook her head. "Tell me why first."

He let out a sigh. Ice crystals formed in the air. "Because we've been busted."

Her heart sank. "Oh, shit."

"I would've called you," he said, "but I was busy clearing out my office."

Her mouth fell open in shock. She couldn't believe what she was hearing. "They *fired* you?"

"No," he said with a shake of his head. "I quit."

"Oh, Sebastian. No." This was all her fault. Well, at least partially, Because she hadn't been able to keep her panties on around him and he hadn't exactly stayed out of them, either. But now he was out of a job.

Her mind spun with possibilities. Maybe they could start up their own firm. Winfield and Stanhope. Had a nice ring to it. Being her own boss would make things easier if she were pregnant.

A cocky half smile suddenly tipped his mouth. "It's not a big deal."

She disagreed. "Of course it's a big deal," she said. "You have no job, Sebastian.

"Not exactly," he said. "Lionel Kane came to see me yesterday to convince me to reconsider. After he promised me your position at the firm was in no danger, I agreed. I spent most of today moving my stuff back into my office."

Joey frowned. Had she heard him correctly? "Wait a minute. *My* position at the firm?"

"Johnson Samuel threatened to fire you."

"That bastard," Joey said with a fair amount of

distain. As if this was all *her* fault? Hanging out her own shingle was starting to sound better and better.

"I'm a partner," Sebastian said with a shrug. "You, my dear, are but a mere associate in their eyes."

"And therefore dispensable." She crossed her arms and let out a short puff of breath in frustration. "Those rat bastards." She stomped her foot for emphasis. She and Sebastian weren't the first two lawyers to ever have an office romance, and they sure as hell wouldn't be the last, either. Thanks to Brooke, she even had the Google stats to support her argument.

Sebastian's chuckle warmed her. "Something like that," he said. "So I told Johnston Samuel and Lionel Kane to take their partnership and shove it."

"But you're still with the firm? You're still a partner?" She couldn't stand it if she were really responsible for his loss of employment. She'd only worked with him a week, but he was a damn good lawyer. He was only thirty-four and already a junior partner in a major law firm.

"Yes," he confirmed.

She let out a long sigh of relief. "So what happens now?" she asked him. "Am I being transferred to another division?"

God, please. Not probate and estate planning.

"Do we have to sign some stupid nonfraternization promise? You should know, I'll refuse to sign."

That made him smile. The one with just a touch of arrogance she found so incredibly sexy.

"Nothing quite so drastic," he told her. "We're both still in litigation, but I'll be concentrating on a new subdivision of the litigation group that will cover med mal and other cases we'll be handling for the county. Bowman's being promoted with a buy-in option after one year. He'll oversee more of the litigation division, but will report directly to me."

"And I'll report directly to Dillard Bowman." She supposed it could be a whole lot worse. Like spending the next ten years drafting wills.

"Exactly."

"I still can't believe you actually quit because they were threatening to fire me." She slipped her arms inside his jacket and looped her arms around his waist. She supposed he had a point, but her pride had taken a direct hit and it stung. She looked up at him and frowned. "They were really going to fire me?"

"Do yourself a favor, sweetheart," he said and drew her closer, skimming his hands down her back. "Blow it off."

He dipped his head and kissed her, taking his time and making her forget about everything but the way his lips moved over hers, the way his tongue teased hers. She'd never grow tired of his kisses, or the way her body came vibrantly alive in his arms. And she planned to spend the rest of her life proving it, too.

Abruptly, she ended the kiss. "Wait a minute," she said, tipping her head back to look up at him. "The firm doesn't handle cases for the county."

He chuckled and that arrogant grin she loved so much fell back into place. "We do now," he said. "That's why Lionel came to see me yesterday. Without me, there would be no business from the county, or Mass General."

"Those greedy rat bastards," she said with much less heat.

Sebastian shrugged. "It's business, Joey."

Maybe so, but that didn't mean she had to like it. She slipped out of his embrace and tucked her hand around his arm. Slowly, they walked toward the house. "How did they find out about us?" she asked him.

He shot her a "get real" look that made her laugh. "Our argument wasn't exactly discreet."

"Oh, yeah," she said with a teasing smile. "You yelled."

He stopped walking. "You yelled first."

She snuggled closer to his big warm body and smiled. "Yes. I do that sometimes."

He shook his head and chuckled. Despite the cold, they resumed their slow stroll toward the house.

"I debated about telling you all this," he said,

"but I figured with the way you flipped when I didn't immediately tell you what was happening with *Gilson,* I'd better not take a chance."

"Smart man," she said, then lifted her lips to his for a quick kiss. He obliged and she felt the tingle all the way to her half-frozen toes.

The kiss ended all too soon for Joey's liking, so she stole another, then another.

He settled his hands on her shoulders to stop her from attacking him again. "There's something else I need to tell you," he said.

He looked all too serious, but she wasn't worried. Not any longer. Sebastian loved her. He hadn't said the words, but she didn't need words when she had actions that spoke volumes. The man had given up his job for her. A position she knew from their conversations was important to him. If that didn't say he loved her, then nothing ever would

"Uh-uh. Me first," she interrupted. "Remember the dare I told you about the other night? Well…"

Standing outside her grandparents home in the freezing cold, she told him how she'd believed the dare she'd drawn was about her revealing the information she'd learned about their mother's past to her sisters. She paused only long enough to gauge his reaction to her telling of the sordid details of Daisy Winfield's secret life, breathing a quick sigh of relief when he showed no outward signs of revulsion. Not that she seriously believed for a moment Sebastian would judge her because of her mother's past, but then again, she'd recently learned that just about anything was possible. Who would've dreamed that a Winfield was one generation away from a ten-dollar hooker?

"But I think I missed the spirit of the dare," she said. "What I told them wasn't what was in my heart, it was what was weighing on my mind."

"Joey—"

"Shhh, let me finish," she said with a frown. "There's a difference, I think. Maybe what I'm supposed to do is trust the people I love with what's in my heart." She reached up and cupped her gloved hand against his cheek. "It's you, Sebastian. You *are* in my heart and I love you. That's the real secret that I've been carrying around."

He opened his mouth to speak, but she gently tapped his lip with her finger to shush him. "I think I fell in love with you from the minute you tried to pick me up with that sorry five dollar bill at the jukebox."

He just stared at her with a big, goofy smile on his face. "Can we go inside now? It's freezing out here."

Playfully, she poked him in his side. "I lay my heart on the line and all you can think about is your own personal comfort?"

He laughed and hauled her close. "I thought it'd be more romantic if was able to say I love you, too, without my teeth chattering."

Her heart soared. God, she loved him so much, and was prepared to spend the rest of her life doing just that. "Even if I'm not pregnant?" she asked, feeling a tiny stab of insecurity.

"If you are, great. And if not," he shrugged, "then maybe we should wait to have a wedding first. Buy a house. That kind of thing."

"Hmm," she murmured, then planted a quick, hard kiss on his lips. She looped her arm through his again and started toward the house. "I've been told a wedding first, baby second, is supposedly the Winfield way. Although I'm sure Grandmother could manage to organize one hell of a shotgun wedding, if necessary. Caterers tremble in fear of her, you know."

As they rounded the corner, Brooke suddenly appeared, nearly colliding with them. "What are you two doing out here?" her sister chastised. "The family has been waiting. Dinner is due to be served in fifteen minutes."

"Kissing and making up," Joey said to her sister.

"So I figured, as did everyone else who's been watching from the window."

Joey looked to the window and laughed,

waving to Katie, Liam and David. "Sebastian. My sister, Brooke."

Brooke extended her hand, which Sebastian shook. "How do you do?"

"Very well, thank you," Brooke replied formally. "Come on. Grandmother is waiting."

"Well," Joey said as the trio approached the front entrance, "are you sure you're up for facing the Winfields?"

"A word of warning," Brooke said as she reached for the latch. "Evil-Lyn is her usual *un*charming self tonight. She's already tried to insult Katie and made a snide comment to Grandmother about your tardiness."

"I hope Grandmother told her to stuff it."

Brooke laughed. "No, but the Admiral came close to whacking her with his cane until David pretended to trip over it."

"Family," Joey whispered to Sebastian. "Can't live with 'em, but couldn't live without 'em." She studied his face, which showed no outward signs of trepidation. The man was a rock. Something, she decided, which wasn't such a bad thing to have on her side. "Are you absolutely sure you're ready for this? We could sneak off for a burger."

"It'll be fine," he said, and hugged her just a little closer. She certainly hoped so, because if there was one thing she was dead certain about it was that her family might always be in her heart, but her soul belonged to Sebastian.

DESPITE SEBASTIAN'S INITIAL apprehension, he actually felt surprisingly relaxed with Joey's family. He'd even survived not-so-subtle interrogations by the grandmother, Evelyn, a lovely woman in her mid-seventies, and the dreaded Great Aunt Josephine. He'd managed to deflect the rather pointed questions about his relationship, or lack thereof, with his absent father from the cousin Joey had called Evil-lyn. The nickname fit, in his opinion.

He didn't know if he'd ever become accustomed to having dinner served by actual servants, and wondered how Joey would feel about dinner with his mom at her small home in South Boston. No fancy fare like he'd enjoyed at the Winfield estate tonight, but whatever his mom served, it'd be hot and good, and eaten at the kitchen table with love, plenty of laughter and casual conversation.

There was nothing casual about the Winfields, with the exception of Joey's sisters. The family was what Sebastian would characterize as politely reserved. The grandfather, whom everyone referred to as the Admiral, was the silent type, but the old gent had an evil eye that he kept shooting Sebastian's way so that it had him wanting to loosen his tie. The old guy wasn't all bad. He had a definite soft spot for his granddaughters, evidenced by the way his stern gaze would light up whenever they spoke with him.

Shortly after dinner, the Admiral excused himself for the evening. The snooty aunt and her obnoxious daughter also left, while the rest of the family retired to a formal sitting room where tea, coffee and a small variety of delicate dessert pastries were served.

Winged chairs and sculpted settees were situated around rosewood tables atop plush white carpeting. A blazing fire roared in the enormous fireplace, tall enough for him to stand inside. According to his mother, he'd once lived in such luxury, but he was too young to remember it, so he never missed it. He'd never craved the Stanhope wealth, but a few bucks sure couldn't have hurt when he was growing up or racking up student loans to get through college and law school. Still, everything he had, he'd earned, and no amount of money could replace the sense of pride and accomplishment he'd achieved on his own.

Beside him on one of the settees sat Joey. She'd worn a sedate black dress that revealed little, but showed off her slim figure to perfection. Her shoes, however, were sparking a particularly interesting fantasy.

"Lindsay should be here," Joey said to Brooke while passing him a cup of black coffee.

"Give it time," her sister replied. "Grandmother told me you'd temporarily lost your wits and practically demanded she invite Lindsay tonight."

"Grandmother exaggerates," Joey said, but sent a quick smile in her grandmother's direction. The Winfield matriarch pretended to pluck an imaginary piece of lint from her sleeve.

"I doubt that," Katie said. "You can be so pissy sometimes, Joey. Really. Someone should warn Sebastian about your temper."

"I don't have a temper," Joey countered.

Sebastian chuckled at that, but wisely kept his thoughts to himself when he received a warning glare from Joey. The grandmother in question sent a sharp-eyed stare in her granddaughter's direction, which Joey pretended to ignore.

"David," Evelyn said, directing her attention to Brooke's date. "Brooke tells us you're returning to the team."

"I've only been invited to training camp, ma'am," David answered politely.

The conversation turned to baseball and predictions of how the Sox would perform in the upcoming season now that David was back on the team. A detail which David refused to admit to, but they all believed otherwise.

Liam, Katie's fiancé, commented on the Patriots win over the Steelers in the previous day's playoff game, followed by varying predictions as to which teams had a chance of making it to the Super Bowl. The Patriots, of course, topped the list of contenders.

"So," Joey said once they reached the carriage house some time later, "were they as bad as you thought they'd be?"

"Who? Your family? They were fine."

"Sure they were," she said dryly.

He followed Joey into the bedroom, where she kicked off her shoes and shrugged out of her coat. "I thought your family was nice." He yanked off his tie and unbuttoned his shirt.

"Ha!" Joey said, as she tugged off her dress. "My Great Aunt Josephine is a snob of the first order. And my cousin Eve has a stick so far up her ass, it'll have to be surgically removed. And if you didn't notice, the Admiral was giving you the look all night long."

Oh, he'd noticed all right. He sat on the chaise and removed his shoes and socks. But it was obvious to him that her family loved her a great deal. He could put up with a snob and stick-up-her-ass cousin if he had to. He'd make damn sure to stay out of range of the Admiral's cane in the future, too.

Naked and unashamed, Joey came to stand in front of him and looped her arms around his neck. "He must've determined you were harmless, or he never would've gone off to bed so early."

Sebastian had his doubts. The man was in his mideighties, but sharp as a tack. He wouldn't have put it past the old coot to have hired Liam and David to keep an eye on him during his absence.

He slid his hands over Joey's curves. "Do we have to talk about your family right now?"

"I thought you liked them."

"I do, but I have a naked woman in my arms and there are so many other things I'd much rather discuss."

He stood and she wiggled closer. "Oooh, like what?"

"Like how much I love you," he said, slipping his arms around her and pulling her tight against him. Her naked breasts brushed enticingly against his chest, hardening him in a flash.

"I do like the sound of that," she said, then lifted her face to his for a kiss.

He kissed her, deeply, soundly and with everything he held in his heart. The heart she'd stolen with one sassy comeback and a sexy glint in her lovely blue eyes.

Two weeks later...

"What do the directions say again?" Joey stared down at the white stick. She gripped the edge of the bathroom counter, afraid to breathe. She was only five days late. Nothing to panic over. She'd never been perfectly regular anyway. Once she'd gone as long as eight days without seeing her period, but she hadn't been in a relationship at the time and hadn't thought twice about being so late.

Sebastian read the insert. "You'll see either a plus or a minus."

Joey let out a frustrated steam of breath. "Yeah, but what does that mean?"

She didn't really believe she was pregnant. She had none of the symptoms, and she'd researched plenty.

God, what had she ever done before Google?

She had no nausea and no breast tenderness. She hadn't experienced a single episode of lightheadedness, either, but she had been tired lately. Although the fatigue could easily be explained since she and Sebastian had spent every single night together since they'd kissed and made up two weeks ago.

He peered over her shoulder. "A plus means you are, a minus sign means you aren't."

"It's blank."

He checked his watch. "It's only been a minute, sweetheart."

It had been longer than that, like just over three weeks, but she didn't need to remind him. In all honesty, until this very moment standing in his bathroom on a Saturday morning waiting for the results, these past couple of weeks, he'd been more concerned about a possible pregnancy than her. No, not concerned, she realized. More like excited by the very possibility they'd created a child together.

Suddenly, he tossed the instructions on the counter, covering the test strip.

Joey gasped. "What are you doing?" She reached to move the sheet of paper, but Sebastian grabbed hold of her hand to stop her.

She attempted to tug to free her hand, but he tightened his grip. "Sebastian?"

He pulled in a deep breath, then let it out in a rush. "Marry me, Joey."

Confused, she looked up at him. The tenderness in his eyes momentarily stole her breath. "Haven't we already had this discussion?" Albeit a casual discussion with no set plans and no date. Just an abstract discussion or two of their future, leaving no doubt in either of their minds that they'd marry—

eventually. She wasn't so old-fashioned to believe she needed a husband to have a baby, but she knew Sebastian felt differently. She understood his concerns stemmed from his own lack of a father, but she'd reassured him countless times, regardless of what happened between them, he would always be a part of his son or daughter's life. If she were pregnant, that is.

He let go of her hand and from the pocket of his khakis, he produced a deep blue velvet box. Carefully, he opened it, revealing a stunning princess cut diamond solitaire engagement ring. "Before we know the answer to what's on the stick, tell me you'll marry me."

"You know I will," she told him. "I love you, Sebastian. You know that."

"I want to know that you'll marry me whether or not you're going to have my baby."

She couldn't help it. She smiled at him. "I think I'm the one who's supposed to be insecure about that sort of thing."

He smiled back at her and wiggled the little jewelry box in front of her. "Yes or no, sweetheart?"

She took the ring box from him and set it on the ceramic tiled counter, then closed the distance between them. Looping her arms around his neck, she pulled him down for a hot, open-mouthed kiss.

When they finally came up for air, she looked into his dark chocolate eyes, filled with love and hope for the future, and whispered, "Yes, I'll marry you, Sebastian Stanhope."

"I was hoping you'd say that," he said, then reached around her and plucked the instruction sheet from the counter.

Together they leaned over and stared at the strip, and little blue minus sign.

* * * * *

THE MARTINI DARES *miniseries concludes*
next month with Lindsay's story!
Look for MY WILDEST RIDE
by Isabel Sharpe,
available February 2008.
Enjoy!

HARLEQUIN®

is proud to present

Because sex doesn't have to be serious!

Don't miss the next red-hot title...

PRIMAL INSTINCTS
by
Jill Monroe

Ava Simms's sexual instincts take over
as she puts her theories about mating
to the test with gorgeous globe-traveling
journalist Ian Cole. He's definitely up for
the challenge—but is she?

On sale February 2008 wherever books are sold.

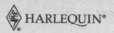